The Muskoka Monster by Patrick James

Book #1 of The Monsters of Canada

Monsters of Canada Book Series

The Muskoka Monster by Patrick James

The Muskoka Monster by Patrick James

It was early in the month of February, in the Muskoka region of Ontario. February the 6th to be exact. It hadn't been the coldest year on the books, but still it was cold enough. The wind was coming out of the northwest and it was gusting up to nearly eighty kilometers an hour. There was some snow and ice on the roads, but it appeared that the snow trucks had been through recently and they had plowed and salted the roads.

It was just after three in the morning and Muskoka Regional Police Officer Kristine Speers was driving west on Highway 118 out of the town of Bracebridge. She had been busy with minor accidents since her shift started at 7pm, or 1900 hours in police speak. Kris, as she was called by her friends, was heading to her favourite sitting spot on the Muskoka River. During the day, and in the summer, she would set up a speed trap there and ruin the weekend fun for drivers rushing to get to their summer homes and away from the noise and

The Muskoka Monster by Patrick James

pollution of Canada's largest city, Toronto. Tonight there wasn't likely going to be anybody travelling down the icy road. Tonight, Kris was not going to set up a radar. No, Kris had already done enough to justify her paycheck for the evening. All she wanted to do was sit and catch up on her reports for the evening, so she didn't have to stay after the shift had ended and do them without getting paid for it.

She looked at the passenger seat and at the thermos full of coffee. She wondered if there was any chance that the liquid would still be hot enough to drink. She doubted it would be, since she had left her home at 6 in the evening. Bringing her own coffee to work was a relatively new thing. It started around a month earlier when the police raided a local donut shop because the night manager had been selling weed and crack cocaine at the drive thru window. Five people in the establishment were arrested, and let's just say that Kris wasn't about to let

The Muskoka Monster by Patrick James

those people handle her food, or her beverages any time soon. She had no interest in drinking the spit of some angry criminal out on bail, awaiting trial and likely going to jail because of her police department. No, she wasn't part of the raid, and yes she was still pissed off about it. Even though she was a thirty year old professionally trained police officer, the Chief of Police did not allow her to go on arrests that he deemed to be too dangerous. It was odd to her because just putting on a police uniform and walking outside of your home could put you in danger. She was in a tough spot, what with her father being the Chief of Police and likely the only reason she got the job in the first place.

Kris pulled into her favourite sitting spot and parked the police cruiser. She kept the vehicle running because it was -12C and she didn't want to freeze to death. Before starting her reports, she picked up the thermos and took off the lid. She smelled the coffee in the thermos. It seemed okay, so she poured half a cup and took a sip. It wasn't hot enough and it made her stomach feel sour almost immediately. It was 3:16 in the morning, and probably too late to be drinking coffee anyway. She opened the door and poured out the coffee. A strong blast of arctic air hit her in the face as she opened the door. It hurt, but it also woke her up a little bit, which was probably a good thing.

Kris closed the door and reached for her laptop when she caught some movement out of the corner of her eye. She damn near had a heart attack when she saw a tall man with long hair and a full beard walk right pass her car. He didn't seem to notice her and just kept walking. With her hand on her service revolver, Kris got out of the car to see what the man was up to. She had to admit, she was feeling a bit nervous, the guy was tall and she was in the middle of nowhere without any nearby assistance if this dude went off.

The Muskoka Monster by Patrick James

She stood and watched the man. She didn't know how it was possible that he didn't see her police car. He had gotten within three feet of the driver side door. With her hand on her gun, Kris was beginning to feel much more confident. She almost hoped this guy was some kind of dangerous criminal, so she could take him down and prove to her old man that she was capable of being more than just some glorified meter maid. She watched without saying anything to the man. He was standing at the edge of the river and just staring blankly down at the running water. They say if you are a police officer long enough, you will see everything, but what happened next, she was not prepared for. The man took off all his clothes and stood there naked in the freezing weather. Officer Speers allowed herself a smile as she made a "shrinkage" joke in her head, but the humour of the situation was quickly lost when the big man started walking into the freezing cold water. Kris realized she was watching a man attempting to commit suicide. Fear shot through her body as she ran towards the man.

"Sir," Officer Speers yelled. "Can I talk to you for a moment?"

The man ignored her and dove into the freezing cold water. Officer Speers got onto the radio and called for backup. She gave her coordinates as best as possible. She explained to the dispatcher that a naked man had jumped into the Muskoka River and she had lost sight of him.

"Ten-four," the dispatcher said. "Paramedics and the fire department are on the way."

Kris ran to the river's edge, determined to get the man out of the water before the cavalry arrived. She wanted to be the hero this time. She ran downstream until she saw the naked man surface for a brief moment. She was certain that the freezing cold temperatures had already taken their toll on the man, and was certain that he was unconscious. She had to get him out of the water and get him out soon, or he was as good as dead. The only way for her to do that was to jump into the frigid water and pull him out. Of course, this meant she had to work fast, or she would be in grave danger herself.

    Kris ran downstream as quickly as she could. She had to get in front of the man's unconscious body and grab him as he came to her and pull him out quickly. She would only have one shot and then she would have to get out of the water. If she missed him, he died. She jumped into the water after taking a deep breath. The water was so cold, it almost took her breath away. The force of the current was enough that it almost knocked her off her feet. She was in good shape, great shape actually, but at 5'8'' and one hundred and thirty pounds, she wasn't exactly a giant and the man that was coming towards her was at least 6'2'' and over two hundred pounds.

The Muskoka Monster by Patrick James

Officer Speers put her hands in the water and braced herself for the big body that was coming towards her. Her hands went numb immediately. She screamed, trying to work through the pain, and waited for the weight to hit her. She thought she was prepared for it, but she wasn't. The force of the collision knocked her off her feet. She grabbed a hold of the man and did not let go, even when her head went underwater. She lost her footing twice and fell pretty hard, but she refused to let go of the man. She took a deep breath when she got to the edge of the river and pulled him out of the water. She got him far enough from the edge of the river and then collapsed.

The wind was blasting down from the north even harder now. Kris was cold and absolutely exhausted. She didn't want to move, but she knew that she had to. The man was not breathing and his skin was turning blue. She knew she had to perform mouth to mouth resuscitation, or this guy was going to die.

The Muskoka Monster by Patrick James

She worked on him for over a minute, rotating between blowing into his mouth and pounding on his chest, and he was not responding. She started wondering if it was too late to save the man. She could hear sirens coming towards her. It sounded like they were a minute, or two away. Kris decided she would keep giving the man mouth to mouth until back up arrived and if he wasn't conscious she would step aside and let the paramedics take over.

"Come on!" Kris screamed out in frustration.

She slapped the man as hard as she could on the chest. He coughed and spit up some water. Kris stopped and looked down at the man. He stared at her for a moment, with a confused look on his face and then closed his eyes. Kris relaxed for a moment, trying to regulate her own breathing, when the man opened his eyes and grabbed for her gun. Kris grabbed the man's hand as he attempted to pull her service revolver from its holster. She just couldn't believe it! Here she was, putting her own ass on the line to save this guy and now he is trying to kill her.

"Let go!" Kris said, as she slapped the man across the face. "I'm trying to help you, asshole!"

"No," the man said. "Kill me, now! Please, I beg you."

"I'm not going to kill you," Kris yelled. "And you sure as hell aren't going to kill me."

"I don't want to harm you," the man said. "I just want to die, I have to die before tomorrow night."

"Why?"

"Because there is a full moon tomorrow night."

"So what?" Kris asked. "Does that mean you are going to turn into a werewolf?"

"Yes, it does," the man said. He tried to pull the gun away from her

The Muskoka Monster by Patrick James

one more time, but didn't have enough strength.

"Sit tight," Kris said. She pulled his hand away from her gun and stood up. A fire truck and an ambulance, plus two police cars, pulled up and parked next to Officer Speers police car. "Help is here."

The Muskoka Monster by Patrick James

2

The man's name was Harry Wilder. Officer Speers found that out when the paramedics were loading him into the back of an ambulance. He had lost consciousness and they had to revive him again and hook him up to oxygen. While they were doing that, Kris went and retrieved the man's clothing and found his wallet in the pocket of the man's jeans.

"Harry Wilder," Kris read. "That's the perfect name for a werewolf."

The paramedics insisted that Kris go to the hospital and get checked out by a doctor too. She had been in the freezing cold water for over a minute and that was certainly long enough to do some serious damage to her. She didn't argue and went to the hospital in Bracebridge. She sat in the emergency room for two hours before seeing a doctor. The doctor took her blood pressure and asked her a few questions before telling her what she already knew, she was fine and could go home.

Kris didn't go home upon gaining her release. She went to the police station to finish her report. The police station was around twenty-five minutes north of the hospital in Bracebridge, in the next town north of it, a place called Huntsville. Both cities were around the same size, with Huntsville having a slight advantage in population. Bracebridge has around 16,000 permanent residents, whereas Huntsville has almost 20,000 people.

Kris liked Bracebridge better. On her first day on the job, back in 2006, there was an incident up in Huntsville that had stuck with her and lowered her opinion on the town. Around noon on a warm day in August, a religious group took to the main street to protest abortions, which is fine, but Kris didn't like the way they did it. The protestors all carried signs that showed aborted fetuses. So, there they were in the middle of the day, walking around with these signs, while people were walking around in town with their children, just trying to do a bit of shopping, or maybe to get a bite to eat while these clowns were standing out on the streets with these disgusting signs. And when any member of the public would approach them and ask them if the disgusting signs were really all that necessary they would simply close their eyes and refuse to answer.

The police were called in and told to park in highly visible spots, but were told not to get out of their vehicle, and not to say anything to the protestors, but to protect the protestors if any members of the public tried to physically remove or attack them. Kris was really offended by the official decision not to do anything. She hadn't become a police officer to just stand there and do nothing, but the mayor and the chief of police, her father, had made the decision and she had to follow orders. Apparently, they were afraid of a lawsuit from this religious group, claiming that their religious freedoms and rights were being restricted. Nevermind the rights of normal, non brainwashed people, they didn't matter and apparently they should have no reasonable expectation that their kids would not have to be subjected to such awful images.

Officer Speers was received pretty well when she got back to the police station. Most of the guys were okay with women being cops, with a few exception of a couple older guys, in their mid to late fifties. One of the younger guys, a kid named Tim Richards asked her to "fist bump" him when she walked into the station.

Kris finished her report around fifteen minutes before her father came in to work. He went into his office, without speaking to her, and then called her to come and see him fifteen minutes later.

The Muskoka Monster by Patrick James

"Why didn't you wait for backup?" Chief Speers asked before Kris could even close the door.

"Because the victim would have died if I had waited," Officer Speers answered. "The doctor that treated me at the hospital told me I saved the man's life. Another minute or so in the water and he would have been dead."

"Okay, fair enough. So based on his suicide attempt and his statement about being a werewolf, he is going to be shipped to the big mental health hospital in Toronto. Why don't you go home and get some sleep. When you come back this evening for your shift, you'll be assigned to transport the suspect down to the city."

"Suspect?" Kris asked, "What is he suspected of?"

"His wife went missing ten months ago and she has not been seen. He came in here shortly after she disappeared saying that they were attacked by a werewolf near Bala Falls during a walk one evening. He claimed that he got away, but he witnessed this werewolf ripping his wife to shreds."

"So, he really is crazy."

"Maybe," The Chief said. "Or maybe he killed her and is working on an insanity defense if we ever find her body. Anyway, go home and get some sleep."

"Yes, sir."

"And good job, Officer Speers."

Kris left the office and headed home. She found it odd that even when they were alone in the office her father would not call her by her name, it was always formal and she dare not ever call him Dad while at work. The shit would hit the fan for sure. She also found it odd that over the last year her old man had decided to start dying his hair jet black, which was nowhere near his natural colour. It looked ridiculous, every time he went

The Muskoka Monster by Patrick James

outside his hair got this bluish tint to it and with his pasty white skin and long skinny body it made him look like a vampire from the 1930s.

It was just after nine in the morning when she got to her home. She lived on five acres, in a three room log home. Her property was located on a dirt road, approximately half way between Huntsville and Bracebridge. It was somewhat isolated, but it was great for sleeping during the day. Too bad that she was so pumped up that she knew she would have a hard time even falling asleep today.

She poured herself a drink and picked up the phone. She called a friend of hers, a man named Rodney to see if he wanted to come over for a quick booty call. He turned her down flat. His wife must have been home. Yes, Rodney was a married man, forty-six years old with two kids. Too bad, Kris thought, the old guy was good in the sack and she needed some stress relief right away.

The Muskoka Monster by Patrick James

   Kris was not a big believer in marriage, or long term relationships. She looked at them as old fashioned and out of date. Plus, as a police officer she had gone to many domestic disturbance calls that were the result of unhappy marriages or commitments. She never understood how marrying another person and treating them like they were your possession was a sign of love.

   She poured herself another drink and thought about who else she could call to come over for some fun. Nobody came to mind. Too bad all the cops she worked with assumed that she was a lesbian based solely on her choice of occupation. She never bothered to correct them, what would be the point, even if they knew she was straight they would never bang the boss man's daughter. Bad career move, if he ever found out. At least that is what they would have thought. Kris wasn't so sure that her old man cared what she did in her personal life, as long as

The Muskoka Monster by Patrick James

she showed up for work on time and in a spotless uniform.

Sleep did not come easily. Kris knew what was going to happen before she even made her way to the basement of the house. She would have some bad nightmares, and of course she did. It's not every day that some crazy man tries to take your gun from you, so that he can kill himself and maybe you too. She slept in the basement bedroom when she worked the night shift just because it was darker down there. Very hard to sleep with bright sun blasting you in the face.

It was a weird life, the life of a cop. Odd work hours, mixed with seeing things a person ought not see. It could be very tough sometimes, but Kris Speers could not imagine doing anything else. Well, she could, but movie star, or astronaut probably wasn't realistic. She liked not being a normal person in a normal Monday to Friday office job, working nine to five. She figured if that was ever the

The Muskoka Monster by Patrick James

life she was forced to live she would just end it all. Growing up, Kris never felt special. With brown hair and brown eyes, she could not compete with all the blue-eyed blondes that all the boys chased. And she was no genius, only of average intelligence, no big university was going to offer her a big scholarship and make her somebody special. No, she was nobody until the day she put on her police uniform. Now, she felt like she finally mattered, at least a bit. She felt like she was part of an exclusive club that got to do and see things most normal people weren't allowed to see.

The phone rang just before 4 in the afternoon, so Kris got up to answer it. It was her father/boss. He wanted her to come in at 6 and pick up an unmarked car to take Harry Wilder down to the city to get a much needed psych evaluation. She agreed to it and hung up the phone. She made a pot of coffee and turned on the local news channel just in time to see her father holding a press conference talking about how well trained his officers are and how he makes sure that he only hires the best of the best. Funny, that he didn't ask her to be at the press conference and tell her side of the story. She would have loved that.

"You're a prick sometimes, old man," Kris said.

She shut off the TV and went to take a shower. She went outside to smoke a cigarette, she never smoked inside the house. The smell of old smoke made her feel sick. It was cold out, around minus twelve and starting to get dark. Kris looked around at the cold winter landscape. The sky was cloudy, and there was a tiny bit of snow on the ground. It was grey and bleak looking. As popular as Muskoka is, and as beautiful as the area was in the summer, most of the big city people, or citidiots as they were called by locals, would never experience how harsh Muskoka could be in the winter. It could also be very depressing.

Kris was feeling depressed lately. She was lonely and yet there was no solution to fix her loneliness. She wasn't going to get married and she had no close female friends. In reality, she had no friends at all, just people she worked with. Maybe a trip down south next month would help her get out of her funk. Maybe some place in the Caribbean. She finished her cigarette and decided to head into work.

She went to the police station and picked up an unmarked cruiser. Her dad wasn't in his office, which pleased her. She had never been that close to him and she still held a grudge that he passed her over three times to hire other people to be police officers, even though they were less qualified than her. One guy, shot himself in the foot on his first day on the job.

It took just over an hour for the hospital to put together the paperwork to release Harry Wilder temporarily to her custody. While she was waiting for it to get done, Kris went into his room and said hello to him. He was restrained to the bed. She held no grudge, or ill feelings towards the man, how could she? He clearly wasn't in his right mind.

"How you doing today, Mr Wilder?"

"So far, so good," Harry answered. "But that'll change in a few short hours when the full moon is at full strength."

"I'm here to transfer you down to Toronto," Kris said. "They are going to get you some help."

"Toronto?" Harry said, "Oh God, no!"

"I'm not a city person either," Kris smiled. "But it isn't that bad."

"You don't understand," Harry said. "The moon will be strong enough for me to turn soon. I don't want to be in this car with you when that happens. The werewolf is not me, I can't control the things he does. I see what he does, I remember what he does, but I just can't do anything to stop it."

"No worries," Kris said. She looked in the mirror on the far wall to see if her badge was straight and if her uniform looked good, you know, just in case there was media outside wanting to do an interview with her. "There is a protective shield between you and me, so wolf out all you like."

"You don't believe me," Harry said. "Can't say I blame you. A year ago I would have thought anybody saying what I am saying to you right now was crazy too."

"I don't think you are crazy, maybe just a bit stressed out. Listen, everything is going to be okay. You aren't facing any criminal charges, they'll just keep you for thirty days and give you some therapy, perhaps some anti-depressants. It'll be good for you."

The Muskoka Monster by Patrick James

"The only way they'll keep me is if their doors are made out of silver," Harry said, mostly under his breath. "This is going to be bad."

Unfortunately, at least for Officer Speers, there were no cameras when she loaded Harry Wilder into the back of her car. He was in a straight jacket, so he wasn't any threat. She loaded him in the back of the car and started driving towards Highway #11. She wondered if traffic was going to be brutal when she got down south, a hundred kilometers or so, to the Barrie area. It would probably be stop and go all the way down to Toronto.

Harry didn't say anything. It was already getting dark and you could see the full moon in the sky. Kris looked in the rear-view mirror. She didn't see a werewolf behind her, just a troubled sad man. She thought about pointing out that the moon was already visible, but decided not to bother. He was mentally ill, it wasn't fair to pick on him.

"Feel like talking, Harry?"

"About what?" Harry asked.

"Your wife," Kris said. "What happened to her?"

"Are you related to Police Chief Speers?"

"Yeah."

"He thinks I killed her and then made up this story about being a werewolf to cover up for it."

"Did you kill her?"

"The werewolf inside me killed her."

"You said that when you turn back into a human, you remember what happened when you were a werewolf, am I right?"

"Yes," Harry said.

"Tell me what happened that night."

"The night my wife died?"

The Muskoka Monster by Patrick James

"Yes."

"We were up by Bala Falls. We went hiking and had a picnic," Harry said. "I was trying to be romantic because I had been trying to convince Janet to have a baby for months. She kept saying no."

"You have any other kids?" Kris asked.

"No." Harry continued, "So, anyway it was getting dark and we were on our way back to our car when Janet turns to me and says let's do it, let's have a baby. I was so excited, I wanted to start right away, so we went and found a really private spot and , you know, started having sex."

"Nice," Kris said.

"It was nice, until I turned into a werewolf and started tearing her apart."

"You remember doing that?"

"Yeah," Harry said. "It was like, so fast, I just don't know what happened. One second, we're just a normal couple in love and the next second I am killing her."

"They never found her body."

"They never will," Harry said. "I ate her."

"Excuse me?"

"You heard me," Harry said. "I tore her to pieces and I ate her whole body."

"I don't really know what to say to that," Kris said.

"I just want to say something," Harry said. "Before tonight happens. The werewolf is not me, I would never hurt you, my wife or any other innocent person."

"Good to know."

"I know you don't believe me," Harry said. "I just want to say, I don't want you to feel bad when you see me turn and you have to execute me. You'll be doing me a favour and you'll be protecting society from an evil creature."

"Okay," Officer Speers said. "By the way, who turned you? Who turned you into a werewolf?"

"I don't remember much about that," Harry admitted. "It was an older guy, I think."

"You think?" Kris asked.

"It's weird," Harry said. "I don't remember the night he attacked me, or how I met him, but I have these dreams that aren't really dreams where he comes and talks to me."

"Dreams that aren't dreams?"

"Yeah," Harry said. "You know how dreams happen in your mind, but they aren't real. These conversations with this guy are in my mind, but they are real, and I am not actually asleep when I am having them. I can't be completely wide awake and he talks to me and gives me advice."

"Like some kind of telepathic connection?" Kris asked. She wasn't sure why she was feeding this guy's delusion.

"Yeah," Harry said. "I don't want to alarm you, but I am starting to feel uncomfortable. I'm getting this sickly feeling that I get before I turn."

"Maybe you should close your eyes and try to relax. Maybe you can fall asleep and avoid turning?"

"It's worth a try," Harry said.

"There you go," Officer Speers said. She felt proud of herself for giving the mentally ill man a way to save face and not have to explain why he didn't turn.

3

Harry Wilder fell asleep pretty quickly. He knew this young police woman didn't believe a word that he was saying and that she was merely trying to humour him, so that she would have somebody to talk to on the long ride down to the city, but he liked her. She seemed like she really did care about his safety and well being. That was rare in young cops these days. Most of them were power hungry little pricks that strutted around like they were heroes, even when they hadn't personally done anything to justify being called one.

Maybe this young woman was right, maybe he could fall asleep and avoid the full moon and not attack and kill her, or anybody else. She was a cute little thing, with the kind of spunky personality that would draw him to a woman back in the day, before he was married. Or before he became a killer werewolf that would tear her body to shreds.

The Muskoka Monster by Patrick James

Last month before he changed, he had convinced himself that he would use the power of his mind to stop himself from turning into a werewolf. It didn't happen. Hell, maybe sleep was the cure.

It's not.

Oh shit, Harry thought to himself. He was adjusting to hearing voices when he was awake, now he was hearing them when was asleep. Well not them, it was really only one voice. In his mind, Harry asked, "Who are you?"

I'm the werewolf. You are going to turn soon. I want you to kill this little bitch.

"I don't want to kill her," Harry said in his dream. "She is my friend."

No, she's a pig. She hates you. She is going to lock your ass up in a nuthouse. Is that what you want?

"I just don't want anybody else to get hurt."

The Muskoka Monster by Patrick James

Well, I am afraid that is not your call. It's time for me to take over. I hope we kill a shitload of people tonight.

"No!" Harry screamed as he awoke from his sleep.

"Harry is everything okay?"

Officer Kristine Speers looked into the back seat of the car just in time to see Harry begin to transform into a werewolf. She almost lost control of the car when she saw him transfer from a normal man to a hideous monster. His face became all distorted, with a long nose and razor sharp fangs. He became covered with a reddish brown type of fur and swelled up to three times his normal size. In other words, he looked exactly like a werewolf.

Kris was in a panic. She was on the highway in the city of Toronto and her prisoner had just turned into a werewolf. He was going wild in the back of the unmarked police car. He was bouncing off the protective shield trying to get at her. Kris gunned the car and tried to figure out what to do. She knew that she had to keep the werewolf in the backseat of the car. Toronto being the biggest city in the country had millions of people that this creature could kill. She couldn't let him get out.

"What the fuck!" Kris yelled. She reached for the radio, but then put it down when she realized she had no idea what she was going to say. Help, my prisoner just turned into a freaking werewolf might not be taken all that seriously. "They didn't teach us how to deal with this bullshit at the academy!"

Officer Speers tried to catch her breath and think quickly. She knew she didn't have much time, the werewolf seemed to be getting bigger. He hit the protective shield so hard that she felt the vibration in the steering wheel. It made her hands hurt. Her first though, was to take out her

The Muskoka Monster by Patrick James

service revolver and shoot the nasty werewolf, but that would also mean she would be shooting Harry Wilder. It wasn't his fault that he was turned into a werewolf and she wanted to help him, if possible.

"Taser his ass!" Kris yelled to herself. "Taser him as many times as necessary until morning comes and the full moon is gone! I hope this doesn't hurt you too, Harry, but I'm going to have to fry this flea-bag until he loses his feisty attitude."

Kris took the next exit ramp off the highway. She needed to find a safe spot to pull the car over and get her taser gun out of its holster. She knew she had to move fast, so she pulled in under the overpass the second she got off the exit. She was reaching down for her taser gun, when she heard a huge crashing sound. She turned to see the rear driver side door being torn off its hinges and the nasty werewolf running away.

"Shit!" Kris yelled.

The Muskoka Monster by Patrick James

She dropped her taser gun on the seat beside her and put the car in gear. She knew she had to stop the werewolf before it killed some random idiot walking down the street. It wasn't going to be easy, the werewolf was moving fast. Kris doubted he could outrun a car. Especially, the way she drove.

The werewolf cut across a field. He was heading right for a heavily populated area. Kris took the first street she could find. She had pretty good night vision, but she knew that if he got too far away from her, she would never find him and people would die.

"No pressure," Officer Speers said to herself.

She reached down and took her service revolver out of its holster. She knew that she couldn't risk just using a taser gun. She didn't want to kill Harry by shooting the werewolf, but she had no choice. Either one man died, or a larger amount died. Harry

The Muskoka Monster by Patrick James

Wilder was a good man, he would have wanted her to protect the people first.

Harry was helpless. He could see everything the werewolf was doing, but had no control over it. He could hear the high powered engine of the police vehicle behind him and he hoped that Kris didn't let the werewolf escape. He hoped that if she got the chance she would shoot to kill. Now that she knew the truth, now that she knew the werewolf was real, Harry was sure that she would do the right thing.

Kris did everything she could do to stay with the werewolf. It wasn't easy. There weren't alot of high speed police chases up in Muskoka. And there sure weren't as many vehicles, or people on the road. She followed the werewolf into an industrial area. She pointed her radar gun at the creature. It was running at over 40km/h. The problem was it wasn't running in a straight line.

"Stay still you hairy bitch!" Kris screamed in frustration. "I just need one clear shot and your problems are over."

Kris never got that clear shot. She followed the werewolf down a long, dark alleyway. She got excited when she saw there was a brick wall at the end of that alleyway. She stopped the car twenty feet from the trapped monster. She had her service revolver in her right hand as she reached for the door handle with her left, but when the werewolf turned and looked right at her, she thought twice about opening the door.

Kris tried hard to work up the nerve to open the door, but before she could the werewolf charged at her car. It gave her an idea. She dropped her gun on the seat and put the car in gear and gunned it towards the charging werewolf. Unfortunately, she forgot to put her seatbelt back on and when the car collided with the big monster, her body came forward as she

The Muskoka Monster by Patrick James

slammed on the brakes. Her head bounced off the windshield only seconds before the driver side airbag exploded into her face and knocked her unconscious. By the time it would take for her to regain consciousness, the werewolf would be long gone.

The collision between the car and the werewolf was so severe that Harry wondered if Officer Speers was still alive. He prayed that she was and that she would be able to catch up to the werewolf and kill it. If not, who was going to stop this creature? He was terrified as he watched the werewolf run towards a residential area. If only there was some way for him to stop this thing.

There wasn't, of course, and no amounting of praying or begging would change what was about to happen. The werewolf ran through several backyards before exiting on a street and running into a local park. Harry screamed in horror when he saw that the werewolf had locked its sights on two people, a young mother and her infant child. The mother was pushing the baby in a blue stroller and never even saw the attack coming.

Harry didn't want to watch. He tried to close his eyes when he felt the werewolf jump into the air. There was no way for him to close the eyes that the werewolf controlled. Harry watched helplessly as the werewolf tore the young mother to pieces before running off with the baby in its evil mouth. Harry hoped that the werewolf would have had enough human flesh for one night and that he might spare the baby. That didn't happen. Harry Wilder watch in horror, completely helpless to do anything to stop the poor baby from being devoured. He would spend the rest of the night with only one thought in his mind:

God, please kill me now. I can't live with this anymore.

4

Officer Kristine Speers would wake up the next morning in a hospital room. It took over an hour for her to be cut out of the vehicle. Police cars were sent out to find her when she did not show up with her prisoner at the mental institution. Her father's face was the first thing she saw when she regained consciousness.

"How are you feeling?" Chief Speers asked.

"Like I was in a car accident," Kris answered. "Where am I?"

"A hospital in Toronto," The Chief answered. "Doctor says you are okay, just a bit banged up."

"Oh," Kris said. She didn't exactly know what to say. How was she going to explain the missing prisoner. "I have to tell you something and I don't even know how to start."

"Let me start," Chief Speers said. "Harry Wilder really was a werewolf."

"Yes!" Kris said. She tried to sit up, but it hurt too much. "How did you know?"

"Security camera from the police car," The Chief said. "I couldn't believe what I was seeing."

"Imagine how I felt!"

"I can't, Kris. I'm just glad you are okay."

"Thanks."

"But we need to have a talk about something important and it can't leave this room."

"Okay," Kris said.

"I didn't know what to do when I saw the security footage, so I called the mayor. He called some federal government agency and shortly after two scary looking dudes from the federal government showed up."

"What happened?" Kris asked.

"Basically, they threatened me, the mayor and you. They confiscated the security footage and told us that we are under strict orders from the Prime Minister's office not to talk about this. He told us that the official story is that Harry Wilder escaped custody with the help of four unknown masked men in a panel van. You were ambushed and rammed by their vehicle and right now there are no leads."

"Fair enough," Kris said. She felt more relaxed.

"Kris," Chief Speers said. "Promise me that you will never speak of this with anybody. If you get married, if you have kids, you never tell them about this. I have a very strong suspicion that if we talk about this we will be killed by some secret government squad."

"No problem, I'll take it to the grave." Kris asked, "But what are we going to do about Harry Wilder?"

"Every police force in Canada is looking for him and all the border crossings have been notified. We'll get him."

"And what happens next month when he turns into a werewolf again?"

"He won't make it to next month," Chief Speers said. "When they catch him, the feds are going to take him into custody and well, you know that they will make him disappear from the planet."

"Poor, Harry. You know, he isn't a bad guy when he isn't wolfing out."

"I know," Chief Speers said. "But you know that he is infected with whatever it is that turns people into werewolves and sadly he has got to be eliminated. It sucks, but taking care of public safety is not an easy job."

"No," Kris said. "It isn't."

"Anyway, you can go home tomorrow. I'm giving you two weeks off with pay, just so you can recover from your injuries."

"I don't think I'll need that long."

"Take it anyways," The Chief said. "We need you to keep a low profile until this thing passes over."

"One more thing," Kris said. Her father was walking towards the door, but stopped when she spoke. "Did he hurt anyone last night? The werewolf, I mean. Do you know if anyone was..."

"Yeah," Chief Speers said. "A young woman and her baby have both disappeared without a trace. Based on footprints where she was last seen, the odds are pretty good that the werewolf killed them both."

"That's terrible," Kris said. "Harry told me that the werewolf doesn't just attack people, it eats its victims."

"I know," Chief Speers said. "Try to get some rest."

The Muskoka Monster by Patrick James

Kris was feeling pretty bad about the young mother and her baby, but not as bad as Harry Wilder. He woke up in a snowy ravine, completely naked and covered in the blood of his two latest victims.

"Why do I believe in you, God? How could you let this happen!"

Harry looked around. He had no idea where he was, but judging from the tall buildings in the background, he was somewhere in the city of Toronto. He was freezing cold, it was well below the freezing mark and he had no clothes on. He wanted to feel sorry for himself, but he didn't have time if he wanted to survive he had to find some clothing, or some shelter.

He decided that he did in fact want to survive. He wanted to talk to Kris Speers, one last time. He hoped that she had survived the crash and that she wouldn't be afraid to talk with him. He knew that he would be dead soon, but Harry just needed to

The Muskoka Monster by Patrick James

vent to somebody that knew he was really a werewolf and not crazy.

The bitch is dead.

Harry ignored the werewolf and started running towards a bridge that was 500 yards away. Why? He could hear human voices. He wasn't sure if his hearing was getting better because of the time he spent as a werewolf, or if it was just a benefit of being in the ravine that voices travelled farther. Harry decided it didn't really matter.

Tall and thin, Harry wasn't really much of an athlete, but his adrenaline was pumping and he moved really fast, faster than he ever moved in his life. When he got closer, he could see that there was a man and a woman under the bridge. The woman, clearly a hooker, based on the way she was dressed and the fact that the very well dressed young man was handing her some money. The man saw Harry running towards them and was not impressed. He yelled at Harry, calling him a crack head and reached down and picked up a piece of ice that he threw in Harry's basic direction. Harry was twenty feet below the couple when this happened. It pissed him off and he charged at the young punk and knocked him off his feet. Harry unleashed all his anger onto this twenty something year old kid and pummeled his face into a bloody mess.

"Take your money and go!" Harry yelled, his voice sounding evil.

The hooker left without saying another word. Harry stopped punching the kid when he heard the werewolf telling him that "the little bastard was dead." Harry didn't care, he was so angry that the God he had always believed in would let the werewolf kill a young mother and her baby, all the while letting this little trust fund douchebag continue to live.

Harry took the kids pants, shirt, jacket and shoes. The pants were a bit short, but pretty close to his size. The shoes and jacket fit perfectly. He looked in the jacket and found car

The Muskoka Monster by Patrick James

keys and a wallet. The wallet had three hundred dollars in it. Harry walked to the street and pressed the alarm panic button. A sporty little German car not twenty feet from where he was started to beep. He shut the alarm off and unlocked the doors with the remote. He started the car and the heater blasted him in the face. It felt great.

Harry knew that the police were looking for him, but he needed food and a beverage. He went through the drive-thru of a local restaurant. if the cashier working the window did recognize him, she hid it well. He knew she hadn't, so he found a parking spot and had his meal as quickly as possible.

What the mother and child weren't enough for you?

"Shut up, werewolf," Harry said out loud. "You ate them not me."

We have something in common now. We are both killers.

The Muskoka Monster by Patrick James

"Guess who I am going to kill next," Harry said.

Yourself?

"No," Harry said. "You."

I doubt that, my friend.

"We'll see," Harry said. He put the car in gear. "Now I need you to stop talking, I have to do some serious thinking."

Sure, buddy. Anything for you.

Harry decided the safest way to get in touch with Officer Kristine Speers would be to call her. He hoped that he could find her home phone number on the internet. His first thought was to look up her address and just head up to her place, but if she was at home she might have other police officers watching her home in case he showed up. He knew that she couldn't have told them about him turning into a werewolf because nobody would believe her and they would probably take her gun away from her if she started talking werewolves.

The pig bitch is dead anyway.

"I told you to shut up, werewolf!" Harry yelled.

Okay, I'll shut up. I won't bother to tell you that there is a cop car behind you. And here you are driving the car you stole from the man you murdered. But, whatever, my lips are sealed.

"Oh shit," Harry said. Looking in the rear-view mirror, he saw that there was an OPP police car right behind him. He was just north of Barrie, Ontario on Highway 11. "Please don't pull me over."

Don't worry about it, Harry. Just kill him, like the blood thirsty son of a bitch that you are.

"You should talk, baby killer!" Harry said, "One day God will make you pay for what you did."

The Muskoka Monster by Patrick James

What will God do to you, murderer?

Harry's heart skipped a beat when he looked in the rear view mirror and the police car's lights lit up. He was trying to decide whether he should run, or pull over when the police car pulled into the left lane and sped by him. Harry exhaled slowly, glad that the cop got another call before he had the chance to run the licence plate of the stolen car Harry was cruising in.

Are you sad you didn't get to kill him?

"Shut up," Harry said to the voice of the werewolf.

Harry was shook up from the near run in with the cop and decided to get off the highway just north of Orillia. He knew the area pretty well and knew there were lots of cottages around this little lake that would be vacant right now. He hoped he could find a place with a computer and internet access, so he could try to look up Kris Speers.

The Muskoka Monster by Patrick James

Good idea. Let's find out where she lives and then we can go kill her. It'll be fun for a couple of killers like us, Harry.

The Muskoka Monster by Patrick James

The Muskoka Monster by Patrick James

5

Harry found a log cabin that was situated down a long drive way. There was no sign that any vehicle had been down the whole street, other than the vehicle he was driving. He hoped it stayed that way. He drove down the lane and hoped it snowed later in the day, he didn't want anybody noticing the fresh tire tracks and coming down to investigating. Especially if they happened to be wearing a badge.

The place was old and rustic. The fireplace was a big stone one and it was a real wood burning one. Harry wasn't sure if it was a smart move to turn it on, but he was freezing cold and there were logs just sitting there waiting to be used. He decided to go for it. The heat sure felt good when Harry finally got the fireplace going.

The log cabin was a two storey home. Harry went upstairs to look around. His investigation revealed the thing he was really hoping to find. In the big master bedroom there was a

The Muskoka Monster by Patrick James

computer and it had internet access. It took three minutes for Harry to get the phone number and address of Kristine Speers.

He wrote the phone number down on a piece of paper and headed back downstairs. He decided not to call until the morning. He wasn't sure if she would be home today, or if she was how many people would be with her. He would try early in the morning. Harry looked around for the remote control for the TV and turned on the twenty-four hour news channel. He needed to know if they were still talking about him.

Of course he was big news. Harry's face was plastered on almost every news channel, even some in the USA. He was flattered, in a weird sort of way. Since when did America care at all about anything going on in Canada? Harry listened to a bunch of so-called "experts" talk about his motivation and what he would do next. It amazed him how wrong these clowns were. The

The Muskoka Monster by Patrick James

only good news to come out of it was when he found out that police officer Kristine Speers was okay and had been released from hospital.

Good, we can kill her tomorrow.

"Not going to happen, werewolf." Harry got up and went to the fridge and found a beer. He opened it up and took a sip. "Feel like talking to me, werewolf?"

What about?

"You."

What do you want to know?

"What's your name?"

I don't have a name.

"Why do you possess people?"

Why not?

"Were you ever a human being" Harry asked.

No.

"So, what are you?"

I'm a werewolf.

"No," Harry said. "You turn into a werewolf when there is a full moon, but you are not always a werewolf."

How do you know?

"Because you talk to me all the time. You are evil, but you are very intelligent. When the full moon comes out, that's the only time you can't talk to me. So what are you the rest of the time?"

A demon.

"I knew it," Harry said.

He fell asleep on the sofa. It was very comfortable in the family room, with the fireplace throwing off so much heat. Comfortable until Harry woke up on the sofa several hours later, completely unable to move. it was like he was paralyzed.

"Oh God," Harry said. "What's wrong with me now?"

"God can't answer that."

The Muskoka Monster by Patrick James

It was a very deep and sinister voice that spoke to Harry. He knew that he had heard it before, but he had never actually seen the person speaking to him. In actual fact, it wasn't a person speaking at all. It was a demon and he got to see it for the first time when it stood at the bottom of the sofa near Harry's feet. It was quite hideous, with grey skin and blood red eyes bulging out of an enormous head.

"The werewolf is my weakest state," the demon said. "But soon, that will not be the case. You want to kill the werewolf, Harry?"

Harry could not speak.

"Of course you do," the demon said. "So, go for it. Kill yourself to kill the werewolf, but you will never kill me. I just want you to know that, Harry. And I want you to know one other thing."

Harry tried to speak, but still could not form words.

"When you and the werewolf are dead and gone, I will still exist and I will rape and torture Kris Speers repeatedly. She will have my baby and then I will kill her. Unless, you leave her out of this, of course. Don't visit that bitch tomorrow and don't ask her what you and I both know you are planning on asking her because if you do her blood is on your hands."

Harry jumped up from the sofa. The fire was still blasting away in the fireplace and Harry was alone. It was just a dream. Harry got up and went into the bathroom. He splashed water in his face and tried to calm down. His heart was racing and felt like it could pound right out of his chest.

"It was just a bad dream," Harry said to himself. "Nothing more."

Wrong, Harry. It was a warning.

"No," Harry said. "It was a bluff. You know exactly what I am going to do tomorrow and you are scared to death.

The Muskoka Monster by Patrick James

You are trying to save your own ass and it isn't going to work."

Okay, Harry. Have it your way, just don't say I didn't warn you, buddy boy.

The next morning Kris woke up feeling very stiff and sore. She made a cup of coffee in the microwave and went outside to smoke a cigarette. She had no idea how she was going to spend two weeks at home. She was already bored to tears. She heard the phone ringing from inside the house and hoped it was her father calling her to ask if she could come back to work early. No such luck.

"Are you okay, Kris?" The male voice on the other end of the line asked.

"Harry, is that you?"

"Yes," Harry said. He was shocked that she recognized his voice so easily. "I didn't think you would know me that quickly."

"I'm good with voices and stuff," Kris said. "Are you okay?"

"No," Harry said. "Are you?"

"I'll survive."

"I need to see you."

"Why?"

"I need your help."

"I'd like to help you," Kris said. "But I don't exactly know what to do."

"I need you to kill me," Harry said. "Before the next full moon. I was hoping you could do it tonight."

"I don't really know what to say," Kris said. "Nobody has ever called me up before and asked me to execute them."

"I'm guessing nobody ever turned into a werewolf in front of you before either."

"Yeah, it's been a week of firsts," Kris said. She held back a laugh. "And some people think country living is boring."

"Will you do it?" Harry asked.

"I really don't want to kill anybody," Kris said. "It's not my thing."

"I really don't want to die," Harry said. "But I will not let that werewolf come back. He killed a woman and her baby."

"I know."

"We can't let that happen again."

"Agreed, but you are still asking me to knowingly kill you, an innocent person."

"I'm a casualty of war, I guess."

"This frigging sucks!" Kris yelled. "Saving your life was the only really heroic thing I have ever done and now because I did that, a woman and her baby are dead and now I have to murder you."

The Muskoka Monster by Patrick James

"I'm sorry."

"My whole career, I've been nothing more than a ticket jockey, a glorified meter maid with a gun, sitting at the bottom of steep hills, so I can catch people speeding, just to generate money for my region. The whole time feeling like a fraud, just wondering when the real action was going to happen so that I could feel like what I do matters."

"Killing the werewolf matters, Kris," Harry said. "You will be a hero. Sure, nobody will know what you did, but thousands of lives will be saved because of you and God will know what you did. That's all that matters."

"Hell, Harry. I don't even believe in God."

"You didn't believe in werewolves either," Harry said. "That doesn't make them any less real."

The Muskoka Monster by Patrick James

"Okay, Harry," Kris said. She choked up a bit as she spoke. "Give me a day, or so, I'm going to need to mentally prepare myself. I assume that since you have my home phone number, you know where I live?"

"I do."

"Tomorrow night, okay?"

"Thanks, Kris," Harry said. "And again, I'm sorry that you got dragged into this."

"Me too," Kris said. "And I'm sorry that you were in the wrong place at the wrong time and now it's going to cost you your life."

"Don't worry," Harry said. "I'm ready to go."

Harry didn't even bother to try to sleep that night. What was the point? he sat outside in the dark and looked up at the night sky. He wondered if there was a Heaven and if there was would they take him. He had killed a man. Still, the events of the previous night were out of his control and the reason why he lashed out. Would God take that into consideration?

Either way there was no point in sleeping. He'd be sleeping permanently soon enough. It was weird, knowing that you were going to die in a few hours. It was even weirder to not be scared about it. But why would he be scared? He wasn't leaving anything, or anybody behind. It was just him. His parents were long dead. His wife's death was much more recent and much more painful. He had no children and no siblings. Harry wondered if his parents, or his wife would be waiting for him on the other side. He had never been that close with his parents, so he doubted they would have any interest in seeing him. His wife? Well, that was hard to say. Maybe she would forgive him for killing her, maybe she wouldn't.

"Guess I'll find out soon enough," Harry said. He looked up at the sky and smiled. "God, it sure is beautiful tonight. You never really take the time to admire the important things when you think you have forever. It's only when you know your time is almost up that you truly appreciate how wonderful nature can really be."

Are you talking to me, Harry?

"Yes, werewolf, I am."

But my time is not almost up, yours is.

"You think you are going to live forever?"

Yes, Harry. I do think I am going to live forever.

Kris Speers didn't have any trouble falling asleep. Sleep was how she handled depression. It always had been her way of shutting out the pain. Some people do drugs, or drink, but that was never her thing. Kris didn't like how it felt to be drunk or high, she didn't like the weird disconnected feeling that came with it.

The Muskoka Monster by Patrick James

In the morning, she woke up and looked at the file she had on Harry Wilder. The homicide detective that was investigating him when he reported that his wife was killed by a werewolf was friendly with Kris and he made her a copy to read through. Harry had no criminal record, neither did his wife. Her name was Janet and she appeared, from her driver's licence photo to be Swedish or Norwegian. Very blonde, with pale blue eyes and very white skin. Quite beautiful. Harry was a handsome man, before he grew the beard and let his hair get long and shaggy. The couple had a combined income of over two hundred thousand dollars last year. Harry worked at home making videos and putting them on the internet. He talked about politics and religion. Kris watched a few of his videos, he was bright and had a good sense of humour. His wife Janet, bought and sold stocks and bonds on the web. Harry had some big cheques coming in from all the advertisers on his videos and Janet would use some of that money to buy and sell the shares of stock.

"Their house in Port Carling is currently worth a cool one point five million, and there is no mortgage on it," Kris carried the file into the kitchen and read it as she made a pot of coffee. "And they have half a million dollars cash in the bank. I feel like a loser, now."

The homicide detective had made some notes. He had interviewed some neighbours and friends and they all said that Janet and Harry were a happy couple. The detective had said that given the couple's good relationship and strong finances, he could find no reason why Harry would kill his wife.

"Because there is no reason," Kris said. "Harry didn't kill anybody. Sad, but after tonight I won't be able to say that."

The Muskoka Monster by Patrick James

6

Kris was still feeling the effects of the car crash and she was on some pretty heavy duty painkillers. It was early afternoon on the day that she was suppose to kill Harry Wilder. She read through the file on Harry twice. She didn't know what she was looking for, really she was mostly trying to keep herself busy. Thinking about killing somebody in a few hours was the last thing she wanted to do.

Eventually, the painkillers kicked in and she couldn't keep her eyes open. She fell asleep on the sofa and had the strangest dream. Actually, it was more of a nightmare. In the dream, she was in her bed sleeping when a loud bang woke her up. She opened her eyes to see a demon standing at the bottom of her bed.

"Who are you?" Kris asks the creature. "What are you doing here?"

"I'm the thing you tried to kill," the demon said. "But you failed and now I am here to kill you."

"I didn't try to kill you," Kris said. "I've never even met you."

"You did try to kill me."

"Please, don't kill me! I'll make it up to you."

"You want to make it up to me?" The demon asked. "Maybe we can work something out and I won't have to kill you right now."

"I'll do anything," Kris said.

"Excellent," the demon said. "You can have my baby."

The demon ripped the blankets off the bed and the clothes off of Kris. He climbed on top of her and started raping her. She tried to push him off, but he was too strong. She closed her eyes and hoped it would be over soon, but it went on forever. Finally, she opened her eyes and what she saw made

The Muskoka Monster by Patrick James

her scream. It was Harry Wilder on top of her, forcing himself on her. More accurately, it was Harry's corpse on top of her, raping her.

"You're getting what you deserve," Harry's talking corpse said. "You brought this on yourself."

The scream woke her up. She jumped off of the sofa and looked around the room. She was alone. For a moment, she wasn't sure if it had been a dream, or not. It seemed so real. She had to look down to see if she had clothes on. She did. Looking out the window, she could see that it was dark outside and she knew that meant that Harry would be showing up soon. She had to calm herself down.

Kris wondered if the government was watching her. She wondered just who in the hell the people that threatened her dad were, but decided she was probably better off not knowing. There was no doubt in her mind that even in peaceful Canada there were secret agencies that performed black ops when necessary and that they would have no problem taking out a ticket jockey like her. She knew was easily replaceable, unlike some of the other cops she worked with that thought the world would fall apart if it wasn't for them telling people to turn their music down.

Harry showed up just after 10pm. He seemed really calm and relaxed when Kris opened the door and invited him to come inside. He went into the living room and sat down. Kris asked Harry if there was anything she could get him. He smiled and remarked that a bullet to the brain would be great.

"I was thinking more like a cup of tea," Kris said.

"Oh, no thanks," Harry said. "I'm good."

"My God, Harry, I can't believe we are going to do this!"

"Me either."

"I appreciate you doing this," Harry said. "I would do it myself, but suicide is against my religion."

"What about trying to drown yourself a couple days ago?" Kris asked.

"I lost my way, I lost my faith."

"Because you couldn't understand how God could let these things happen? How could he let innocent people be killed by werewolves, or turned into them?"

"Yes."

"I ask myself those kinds of questions all the time," Kris said. "Of course, I never had any faith to lose."

"Last night I was really scared and felt alone. I couldn't sleep, so I started reading The Bible and it lifted me up."

"Okay," Kris said. She didn't want to express her real opinions.

"Anyway," Harry sensed her skepticism. "When I stopped reading, I actually managed to fall asleep for a few moments and God came to me. It was amazing. He told me that I was very brave and that because I am doing the right thing, there is a place in Heaven for me."

"I hope it was real and not just a dream."

"It was real, Kris." Harry said, "Just remember what I am telling you now, that if you need help you can ask God and he always helps if you are a good person."

"Really."

"Yes," Harry said. "And you are a good person."

"I don't feel like a good person right now."

"You are." Harry said, "There is no doubt in my mind."

"Except that by killing you I am breaking both the law and the ten commandments."

"You are killing evil, not me. A demon that has no right to be in this world. And, I am giving up my life willingly because like you I want to do the right thing."

"But people are going to think you were evil," Kris said. "Doesn't that bother you?"

"No, it doesn't matter what people think. God knows the truth and so do those that care about me."

"I guess."

"I hope we see each other again," Harry said. "In Heaven."

"Me too." Kris said, "I hope there is a Heaven."

"There is."

"Okay," Kris said. "But before we do this, are you sure there is no way we can find a cure?"

"Yes, I'm sure. Who would we even ask?"

"My dad said that these government officials came and talked to him and told him not to mention werewolves to anybody, or else."

"So?"

"So, it sounds like high ranking government officials know that the werewolf is not a made up thing. If they know werewolves exist, maybe they know of a cure."

"Turning me over to those type of people would be a bad thing for me," Harry said. "Best case scenario is they kill me. Worst case scenario is they conduct a bunch of really weird experiments on me and then kill me. I'll pass."

"Okay, fair enough," Kris said. "What about this, we find the guy that made you and we kill him. I always see in werewolf movies that if the creator dies, the infected person is freed of the curse."

"Couple problems with that," Harry said. "First one, I have no idea who the guy is, nor where I can find him. Second problem, just because he made me that doesn't necessarily make him evil. He could just be another person in the wrong place at the wrong time who was turned against his will."

"True," Kris said. "You know, Harry, you really are a good person."

"Thanks," Harry said. "Should we do this thing now?"

"I guess."

"How should we do it?" Harry asked. "Should we make it look like I broke in here looking to kill you?"

"That's what I was thinking," Kris said. "Go outside and I'll lock the door. You kick it in and I'll shoot you."

"You got your story straight for the authorities?" Harry asked. "I don't want to get you into any trouble?"

"I'll be fine," Kris said. "Right now you are an escaped felon with a grudge."

"Okay," Harry said. He stood up. "Let's do this."

"I hate this," Kris said. She went into the kitchen and took a gun out of one of the drawers. "I'm sorry it has to come to this, Harry."

"Thanks," Harry said. "It's for the best. I just hope I can kick in the door, I've never done anything like that before."

"You'll be fine," Kris said. "Just put your weight into it."

And that's what Harry Wilder did. It took him three kicks to get the locked door open and to get back in the house. He charged at Kris and she shot him dead with one bullet right between the eyes.

"Rest in peace, Harry." Kris said, "I hope you are right and there is a Heaven."

The Muskoka Monster by Patrick James

7

It only took a few hours of basic questioning before the coroner's office was allowed to move the body of Harry Wilder. It was quickly ruled as a cleaning shooting and Officer Speers was cleared of any wrongdoing. When everybody else had left, her father, Chief Speers took her aside and asked her if Harry had contacted her and asked her to help him put an end to the werewolf. She told him the truth.

"Fair enough," Chief Speers said. "But I have to tell you, prodigal now forces me to make you see a shrink before allowing you back to work. You'll be off for a minimum of sixty days, but don't worry you'll get paid."

"Thanks."

"You helped a man tonight, you must feel good about that."

"Not yet," Kris said. "Not yet."

The Muskoka Monster by Patrick James

Kris slept away most of the next two days. On the third day she had her first meeting with the department appointed shrink. The woman worked from her home in the village of Dorset. She seemed nice enough and quite reasonable, but Kris found the whole experience to be a complete and total waste of time. It wasn't like she could talk about anything real. She imagined what the doctor would have thought if Kris told her the truth about Harry Wilder being a werewolf. Pretty much guaranteed her police career would be over. Hell, she wouldn't even be able to get a job as a poorly paid security guard if she started talking about monsters.

An interesting thing happened that morning. Kris looked out her window to see what the weather was like and she saw a red sedan sitting in front of her house. It had a government feel to it and Kris wondered if some secret government agency was keeping tabs on her. When she left the shrink's office she saw the car again. It was sitting

The Muskoka Monster by Patrick James

in the parking lot of a restaurant on the main street of Dorset. Kris was stopped at a red light because of a one way at a time bridge that went through the main part of town. It grabbed her attention right away when she saw the car because the restaurant was a seasonal business that was only open during the busy summer tourist season. Kris thought about confronting the driver, but she wasn't in uniform and did not have her weapon, or police radio with her. Plus, it would be stupid to confront some government ninja anyway.

When the light turned green, Kris gunned it across the bridge and pulled over in the parking lot of the liquor store. She waited for fifteen minutes to see if the red sedan would follow her, but it didn't. She was both relieved and disappointed. She really didn't want to go home, it wasn't much fun being in the place where she had to gun down an innocent man. Kris decided to go get a coffee and find a place to park.

The Muskoka Monster by Patrick James

Places to park were easy to find in Muskoka during February. It was snowing again and the weather lady on the local radio station had just said that it was minus twenty outside. Kris was not bothered by the cold at this point in time. Her mind was racing and she had no idea how she was going to get her life back on track. How do you get over pulling the trigger and taking a life, even if it was the right thing to do, the only thing to do.

"I have to sell the house," Kris said. "There is no way that I can live there anymore."

Kris went home and called a realtor and set a meeting up for the next day. The agent would come over in the morning and tell her what the house was worth. She had a hard time sleeping that night and was up three hours before the realtor showed up.

The realtor was a woman name Gail Wheaton. She stood about six feet tall and was wearing high heel shoes that

The Muskoka Monster by Patrick James

made her even taller. It was awkward for Kris because the woman was so tall that she was looking right into her breasts when they stood face to face. And they were some really large fake breasts that the realtor had.

She also had a big ass purse that contained two dogs. Gail informed Kris that she took the two dogs with her everywhere. Apparently, Gail thought she was living in Hollywood.

"Nice," Kris said. She looked at the dogs. "What are they, pugs?"

"No," Gail said. She reached into the purse and pulled the dogs out and held them in front of her enormous breasts. "They are jugs.

"They certainly are," Kris said, trying hard not to laugh. "Two good sized jugs, right there."

"I know," Gail said. "I didn't think they were going to get this big."

The Muskoka Monster by Patrick James

"Really," Kris said. She could no longer look directly at the woman. Glancing sideway, she said, "How much does one of those bad boys weigh?"

"Probably about ten pounds."

"They are very healthy jugs."

"A little smaller would have made them easier to carry around."

"You don't have to tell me," Kris said. "If I tried carrying around two big jugs like that I would throw my back out, or something."

"Anyway," Gail said. "I noticed that your property is not on water. That is going to hurt resale value a bit. City people come up here looking to be right on the water."

"Okay."

"Do you mind me asking why you want to sell?"

"Because I shot and killed a guy right where you are standing."

The Muskoka Monster by Patrick James

"Excuse me?" Gail said. "Did you say you shot and killed somebody in here?"

"I did." Kris asked, "Do you think that will hurt resale value?"

"Probably," Gail said. She put the two dogs back into the purse. "So, you're the cop that I heard about on the news?"

"I am."

"I'm sorry you had to go through that," Gail said. "Anyway, I'm going to go back to my office and I'll look up some comparable properties and I'll get back to you with what I think might be a fair price for this home."

"Great," Kris said. She watched the woman walk away with her two big jugs and get into her car. "I should have asked her what she named those two bad boys. Maybe Righty and Lefty, or Massive and Tits."

Kris laughed at her own joke, but the laughter quickly stopped when Gail

The Muskoka Monster by Patrick James

Wheaton pulled away from the house in her car. Kris watched as the red sedan from down the street followed behind her. She wondered if Gail was in any danger and if she should call the police. What would she say? As far as she knew, the driver had not broken any laws and if they were some government agency, it might be smarter to pretend that she didn't know they were following her.

"If they are a government agency," Kris said to herself. "They are pretty sloppy. You'd think they would switch up cars and try to be less obvious. Unless, they want me to see them. Maybe it's like a threat, we are watching you, so you best keep your big mouth shut."

Turns out Kris worried for no reason, the realtor was okay. She called the next day and Kris went into Gail's office and signed the papers to list her house. She sat patiently through a speech about how the house was valued. She wasn't really that interested and didn't care how much the house sold for she just wanted out. And she was happy that Gail had not been harmed by the person, or persons, in the red sedan.

Her happiness was short-lived, though. Kris came out of the real estate office only to find that the red sedan was parked across the street from the office. She decided it was time to confront the driver, enough was enough. She looked right at the car and made her way into the street. She had to wait until a yellow school bus passed by before running across the street. The driver saw her coming and started up the car and drove away before Kris could see who it was behind the wheel. She would not see the red sedan again, until the night before the next full moon.

The Muskoka Monster by Patrick James

8

It was the 8th of March, the night before the full moon. Kris Speers was back in the village of Dorset, paying a visit to the shrink. Therapy wasn't helping Kris at all. Asking her how she felt about ending another person's life over and over again seemed to be quiet pointless to Kris, but sadly it was the shrink's go to move.

"It feels like shit," Kris would say over and over again. "But it was me or him."

She left the hour long appointment and made her way back to her car, which was parked on the side of the road. Kris was sitting in the car, with the engine running, waiting for the car to heat up and the windows to defrost when the red sedan drove by her. She looked up at the last second to see the car coming towards her and watched as it passed by. She never got a chance to see the licence plate and really wasn't that interested in going after the car to get it.

The Muskoka Monster by Patrick James

"They know where I am if they want me," Kris said.

She started driving towards her house. A few minutes into the drive, she saw the red sedan driving up behind her at a high rate of speed. Kris kept driving, suddenly curious to see what was going to happen. What the driver of the car didn't seem to get was that after you witness a man turning into a werewolf in front of you, it is hard to be scared of much after that.

The red sedan followed Kris right to her house and pulled right into the driveway right behind her. It seemed that the driver had finally decided they wanted a meeting. Kris got out of her car and calmly tapped on the glass of the driver side window of the other car. The window came down and Kris finally was face to face with her stalker. She couldn't believe who it was.

The Muskoka Monster by Patrick James

"Do you want to get in?" The driver asked. "I think we need to talk."

"Sure," Kris said. She walked around and got into the passenger seat of the red sedan. "So, you've been following me for a long time."

"Yes."

"You want to talk to me about something?"

"I do."

"About Harry Wilder?"

"Yes."

"So talk," Kris said.

"Maybe I should introduce myself first."

"Not necessary," Kris said. "I know who you."

"You do?"

"Yes."

"So, you killed Harry?"

"I did," Kris answered. "I had no choice, he would have killed me if I hadn't killed him."

"It's okay, Kristine. You don't have to lie to me, I know the truth."

"What truth?"

"That Harry was a werewolf and that he asked you to kill him before he turned again."

"I don't even know what to say to that," Kris tried to laugh off the comment.

"Kris, I was married to the man. I know he was a werewolf."

"Is that why you are here, Janet? Do you want to harm me to get revenge for Harry?"

"No," Janet Wilder said. "I'm here to help you."

"Help me with what?" Kris asked.

"Help you keep Harry dead."

"I don't understand."

The Muskoka Monster by Patrick James

"Did you go to Harry's funeral, Kristine?"

"No."

"Would you happen to know if his body was cremated?"

"It wasn't," Kris said. "It was a closed casket ceremony."

"That's too bad," Janet said. Worry came over her pale face and Kris saw fear in her big blue eyes. "It would have saved us a whole bunch of trouble."

"How's that?" Kris asked.

"The next full moon is tomorrow."

"Yeah," Kris said. "So?"

"Harry hadn't been a werewolf for long and I guess he just didn't know everything."

"What do you mean?"

"I mean tomorrow night Harry's corpse is going to turn into a werewolf and he is going to dig his way out of his grave and kill the first person he sees."

"You're shitting me!"

"No," Janet said. "I wish I was."

"Great," Kris said. "How do you know all this?"

"I did a lot of research, trying to save Harry."

"Wait a minute," Kris said. "Harry told me that he killed you. He told me that he was banging you in a field up near Bala Falls and that he turned into a werewolf and killed you."

"You have a way with words," Janet said. "But that didn't happen."

"What did happen?"

"I'll tell you some other time," Janet said. "If you do me one favour."

"What?"

"Sit in the cemetery where Harry is buried and put a bullet in his head when he turns into a werewolf and digs his way out of his coffin."

"I feel sick," Kris said. She buried her face in her hands. "It was tough enough to do it once, now you come here and ask me to do it again."

"Sorry," Janet said. "But there aren't too many people I can ask to do this."

"Why not do it yourself?"

"Because I have never fired a gun before and I am afraid that if I miss the werewolf will get away and kill somebody."

"Fine," Kris said. "Anything else I should know?"

"Yes," Janet said. "The old movies have it right, you can only kill a werewolf with silver or fire, nothing else will work."

"Where the hell am I going to get silver bullets?"

The Muskoka Monster by Patrick James

"There's a gun in my glove box, already loaded. Take it."

"Okay," Kris said. She took the weapon out of its resting place and looked at it. "Anything else."

"Yes," Janet said. "Don't miss, make sure he is dead. Werewolves aren't dead until they spontaneously combust and turn to ash. A good head shot, or shot to the heart will do it."

"Okay."

"If he doesn't turn to dust, he isn't dead."

"Got it."

"I can't stress this enough, he must die before the full moon is over, or else we will have way bigger problems than a werewolf."

"What the hell does that mean?"

"It's a long story," Janet said. Kris noticed she was starting to tear up. " A real long story."

The Muskoka Monster by Patrick James

"I've got time, if you want to talk," Kris said. "Seriously, I have absolutely nothing to do."

"Really?"

"Yeah, not until tomorrow night anyway," Kris said. She tried to smile to lighten up the situation. "By the way, I'm really sorry about Harry. This must be so hard."

"You have no idea," Janet said.

"So, why don't you come inside my house and we'll have a drink and talk," Kris said. "It might help you, it'll definitely help me."

"Is that the house that Harry died in?" Janet asked.

"Oh geez," Kris said. "I'm sorry. If you want there is a pub down the street. It won't be busy this time of year, we'll be able to talk openly."

"Okay," Janet said. "Let's go there."

They drove to the pub in silence. Once inside, Janet ordered a glass of red wine, so Kris said she would have the same thing. She really didn't know what to order, drinking wasn't her thing. They found a booth in the corner, well away from the other two customers that were sitting at the bar.

"Do you know what a dead is?" Janet asked. She sipped her glass of wine.

"A dead?"

"Yes."

"No."

"A dead is a type of monster," Janet said. "The type of monster that Harry will become after the full moon tomorrow night, if you don't kill him while he is in werewolf stage."

"Okay," Kris said. She took a sip of wine. She didn't care for it, but didn't say anything. "So, you are saying that Harry's corpse will turn into a werewolf tomorrow night and then after the full moon is over he will turn into another type of monster called a dead."

"Yes."

"What does a dead look like?"

"Like a regular person, until it gets mad," Janet said. "When it gets mad its eyes turn yellow and it gets fangs like a vampire."

"So," Kris said. "A dead is like a vampire."

"Not at all," Janet said. "A dead is not like a vampire, for one thing a dead can go outside in the daytime. Vampires can fly, deads can't. Vamps are technically stronger, but deads are still way stronger than human beings."

"So vampires are real too?"

"That's what they tell me," Janet said. "But I have never seen one."

"Shit."

"Deads have one huge advantage over any other monster I know of."

"What's that?"

"They are immortal."

"So are vampires."

"No," Janet said. "Not really. I mean, vampires can live for a long time, but they can be killed with fire."

"And a wooden stake," Kris added.

"No," Janet said. "That's just Hollywood fantasy. Fire is the only thing that kills vampires. Nothing kills a dead."

"For real?"

"For real," Janet said. "A dead's only weakness is during the full moon when it turns into a werewolf."

"So even after Harry turns into a dead, he'll still turn into a werewolf on the night of the full moon?"

"Yes," Janet said. "But hopefully Harry will never turn into a dead because you will stop that process from happening tomorrow night."

"So, that's why you are so stressed," Kris said. "Because if the werewolf isn't stopped tomorrow, it'll be an immortal and unstoppable monster for a full month."

"Yes," Janet said. "Deads can be slowed down, but they will always regenerate, even if you turn them into ashes with fire. You can buy yourself time, but that is about it."

"I guess I have no choice, but to stop him."

"If you don't," Janet said. "He'll come after you."

"Harry liked me."

"But the werewolf didn't," Janet said. "Or should I say the dead didn't."

"Harry use to tell me that the werewolf talked to him, he could hear him in his head."

"Not the werewolf," Janet said. "The dead. Werewolves are mindless creatures. Let me ask you something, did you have any dreams about a creature coming to visit you?"

"I did," Kris said. "It looked like a demon."

"Well," Janet said. "I've got some bad news for you, that was the dead. You saw him for what he really is, it was a dream visit, but not a dream."

"What's the difference?"

"Dreams aren't real, his visit was. Did he threaten you?"

"Yes."

"So, that demon you saw isn't what the dead will look like, if you don't kill the werewolf. The dead will look exactly like Harry, until it gets mad."

"Yellow eyes and vampire teeth," Kris said.

"Yup."

"Okay, I get your point," Kris said. "I'll take care of it."

"Good."

"Say," Kris said. "Do you want to come with me?"

"No thanks," Janet said. "I'll come visit you the next morning."

"I could use your help."

"No, I'd be useless, plus I think you need to stay focused. The moon will be at full strength at 9:42pm. He should be out within ten minutes of that time. Please don't miss, or he'll tear you apart."

"Gotcha," Kris said. Suddenly, she felt like having another drink. "I killed him once, I guess I can do it again."

The Muskoka Monster by Patrick James

The Muskoka Monster by Patrick James

9

Kris knew she was dreaming. In the dream she was in her bedroom, standing there with no clothes on. She walked down the hallway to the bathroom. As she entered the bathroom, she noticed that the shower was running. The red shower curtain was closed and it was steamy. She pulled back the shower curtain and saw Harry Wilder standing there. She climbed into the shower and he put his arms around her. The pair started to kiss. He was extremely passionate and seemed to enjoy feeling her up. She enjoyed it to, at least until the moment he turned into a werewolf and sank his fangs into her throat. She woke up screaming.

"Holy frigging shit!" Kris said, "I hope that's not some kind of freaky premonition."

The phone rang, so Kris went and answered it. She knew who it was, the shrink's office reminding her of her appointment tomorrow afternoon. They had already reminded her yesterday, when she was there, but she knew they would call her again. They always did. She figured it was a money thing, one of the patient's there had told her that therapy was two hundred dollars an hour. Kris was thankful she wasn't paying for it.

She was also getting kind of sick of going all the way to Dorset. She didn't see the point of it because as every week went by she became more and more convinced that she would never be a police officer again. In her mind, she could not imagine them allowing her back on the force after having a prisoner escape her custody and then having her shoot that prisoner to death while off duty. If something else happened, she could only imagine the lawsuits that would be filed.

"I'm going to have to get another gig," Kris said. "Too bad I have no skills. If I had of known that it paid two hundred bucks an hour, I might have considered becoming a shrink myself."

The Muskoka Monster by Patrick James

Kris wasn't happy to be up so early. She had deliberately stayed up late the night before, so that she could get up late and just go do what she had to do. Now, she was up early and she had nothing to do but sit around all day and wait for nightfall.

"Harry would want me to finish the job," Kris said. "He wouldn't want me to bail on him now. The idea was to stop the werewolf and that is what I am going to do."

It was a long day and time just dragged by. Kris kept going outside to smoke a cigarette and by the early evening she had smoked over half a pack. She wondered if the reason most people smoked so much was boredom. She had a shower and got ready to head out to the cemetery. She wanted to get there a little bit early because she had no idea how big the place was and she also needed time to find Harry's plot.

She had the gun that Janet gave her on the passenger seat beside her.

The Muskoka Monster by Patrick James

All the cops she worked with knew her car and there was no worry that she was going to get pulled over. As she drove, she found it hard to focus. She wasn't scared, she was just slightly overwhelmed. She thought about this creature that Janet had talked about called a dead. She wondered why she never heard of it before. Sure, most people think that werewolves are creatures of fiction, but they have still heard of them, not to mention vampires, demons, and zombies. How come nobody writes made up books about these deads?

Janet seemed like she was a decent and honest person, but Kris had to admit that she really didn't know her. It was weird that she wouldn't talk about how she survived Harry attacking her when he turned into a werewolf. Kris felt like she owed her the whole story, especially when she had the nerve to ask her to go and kill the werewolf. Keeping secrets in times like this could lead to very bad things.

Of course, Kris had no choice but to go and kill the werewolf. If deads were real things, she would be in danger if this indestructible creature came after her. The biggest fear that Kris had was that these creatures, these deads, weren't real and Janet was sending her on a wild goose chase because she was having some kind of nervous breakdown because her husband had turned into a werewolf and tried to kill her.

"Or maybe she is setting me up to kill me out of a need for revenge," Kris said. "Werewolf or not, Harry was her husband."

Kris decided it was not likely that Janet was setting her up. They had spent enough time together that Kris knew she wasn't likely a threat. Plus, if she really wanted to she could have killed Kris back at her house. Nobody was around. Also, it didn't make sense to Kris that you would hand somebody a loaded gun if you had plans to kill them. Especially a trained police officer who was very skilled with a weapon.

    Kris got to the graveyard about ten minutes before nine. It was a very cold evening. Her car was the only one in the parking lot. Janet had said the full moon would be at full strength by 9:42, so Kris expecting to be shooting the werewolf by around ten o'clock. That helped her deal with this awful situation, to think that it would all be over in about an hour.

    The cemetery was old and rather large. It took her twenty minutes to find Harry's grave. Kris had the pistol in her waistband, covered by her winter coat. Not that it mattered, she was the only person in the empty graveyard. The temperature was well below the freezing mark and Kris was in a bit of pain. Mostly her feet were bothering her.

    "Time sure drags when you are slowly freezing to death," Kris said to herself. "Come on werewolf, I need to get the hell out of here.

The Muskoka Monster by Patrick James

The werewolf never came. Kris stood there until almost ten o'clock and nothing happened. At first, she was afraid that she had misread the tombstone, but a quick recheck did reveal that she had the right grave. At ten, Kris made her way to the car. She just couldn't take it anymore, it was so cold and she could not feel her hands or feet.

Back in the car, she blasted the heat and relaxed. It was painful when her hands and feet started to thaw. She cried out in pain, just to get it out of her system. Once the feeling came back to her fingers, she thought about going back to the grave, but decided against it. There was no sign that the grave site had been disturbed and she had not seen a werewolf come running out of the cemetery since she had been sitting in the car.

"Janet has some explaining to do," Kris said. "Although, I'm glad there was no encounter with a werewolf, or a dead tonight. One time is one time too many."

Kris put the car in gear and drove home. When she got home, she put a log in the fireplace and lit it up. She smoked a cigarette inside the house, she just wasn't going to go stand outside anymore tonight. After an hour or so, Kris fell asleep on the sofa and didn't wake up until the next morning.

"Ouch," Kris said, as she sat up. Her neck hurt from sleeping in an awkward position. "Must have coffee."

She went into the kitchen and made a pot of coffee. She made it really strong, even though she had nowhere to go. Kris needed a boost and she knew it. It had been a long and tough winter, like every Canadian winter was, but this one was different. She was really struggling with depression now. Her job was her identity and without it, she saw no reason to even bother getting out of bed.

The Muskoka Monster by Patrick James

Today, though, she did have a reason to get out of bed. She wanted to confront Janet Wilder on her wild story. She walked over to the kitchen table where she had left her phone and called Janet. She answered on the third ring.

"Is it done?" Janet asked.

"No."

"Did you say no?"

"Yes, I did."

"Oh God," Janet said. "What happened?"

"Nothing happened."

"What do you mean?"

"I stood in the cemetery for almost an hour after the full moon," Kris said. "And the werewolf never came."

"Are you sure?"

"Yes," Kris said. "I'm sure. I would have noticed a werewolf digging its way out of a grave."

"Oh no," Janet said. "Kris, I need you to listen to me..."

"Last time I listened to you I ended up standing in a graveyard, freezing my ass off for no reason."

"Kris, please! I need you to listen and not talk. You need to get out of your house right now and come to my house. I will send the directions to your phone."

"I don't think so," Kris said. "I've had enough adventure for one day. I think I am going back to bed."

"Kris, please get out of the house!"

Kris hung up the phone without reply. She had no interest at all in listening to any more of Janet's crazy stories. As far as she was concerned, Harry Wilder was dead and that was that. Her opinion soon changed when she turned around and saw him standing six feet from her.

"Hello, Kris," Harry said. "I think we need to talk."

The Muskoka Monster by Patrick James

10

Janet got dressed as quickly as she could and ran for her car. She knew exactly what must have happened. Somebody had moved Harry's body, so that he could turn and become a dead. She had no idea who would do such a thing, but at this point in time it really didn't matter, her number one priority was to save Kris Speers from the dead that was coming for her.

Janet was in a panic. She was driving too fast for the icy weather conditions and knew she had to slow it down. It was a forty minute drive from her house to Kris's place. Her stomach was in knots the whole trip. It didn't get any better when she pulled into the driveway and saw that Kris's car wasn't there. Janet jumped out of her car and ran into the house.

The front door was not only unlocked, but it was open. Janet ran into the kitchen. There were obvious signs of a struggle and there was blood on the floor. Janet fought back

The Muskoka Monster by Patrick James

tears as she frantically ran from room to room looking for Kris. She wasn't there. The only good news for Janet was that she didn't find a body. Kris might still be alive.

"What the hell!" Janet said, "I've got to find her and I have no idea how."

Janet drove around the area Kris lived in, hoping that she would find her alive wandering the streets. Yes, she knew that she was just grasping at straws, but there was nothing else she could do. She knew that if the dead that now possesses Harry's corpse was in the house, there was no chance of any human being getting away from it. Yet, here she was aimlessly driving around looking for a girl that was more than likely already dead.

"No," Janet said to herself. "I must act as though she is alive until I have proof that she is dead."

Janet drove to the cemetery. She wasn't really sure why, but she had to do something. When she got there, she made her way to Harry's plot. It took a few minutes to find it, but when she did she knew that she had been played all along. She looked down at the ground and saw that it was solid and the grave had not been disturbed since it had been first filled in. During the winters in Canada, the only graves that can be used are ones that have been dug out during the good weather. When the person is buried, the plot is filled in with dirt and grass is placed over it in the spring.

"Harry was never in the coffin," Janet said. She remembered Kris saying something about it being a closed casket ceremony. "Somebody took his body out of the coffin and hid it somewhere so that he could turn into a dead."

The question was, who would do such a thing and why would they do it. That was something that Janet didn't know. It was possible that it was another dead, but seemed unlikely.

The Muskoka Monster by Patrick James

Deads were solo creatures. They knew when they were looking at one of their own and they never really fought with each other, but they wouldn't work together either. They respected each other and didn't interfere with each other's lives.

So, who did it? Who took Harry's body? Was it those government agents working for some secret agency? Did they take Harry's body for some secret experiments, or something? And if they did, are they still alive? Did Harry kill them? Does anybody from this government agency know where the dead is now and do they know if it has Kris? Do they have any ideas on how to get her safely away from him, and just who the hell are "they" anyway?

"That's a lot of questions," Janet said. "Questions I don't know if I will ever find answers for. I am so sorry, Kris, but I don't know how I am going to be able to help you."

Kris was in some serious need of help too. She woke up to find that she was naked and covered in dry blood and locked in a cage. She appeared to be in a basement. She stood to her feet and looked around. There was another cage about ten feet from her. It was empty. She heard a noise coming from behind her and turned to see Harry standing there. Well, not Harry exactly, but the dead that looked like him. He was also naked.

"I'm sorry I had to slap you around," Harry said. "But you left me no choice. I told you that you were coming with me and I meant it."

"Fuck you."

"Classy bitch, ain't you." Harry asked, "Do you want to know why you are still alive?"

"Fuck you."

"I'll give you a hint," Harry said. "It's the same reason why you are naked."

"I helped you and this is what you do to thank me."

"No, you helped Harry to stop me. I know it gets confusing when you are looking at him, but I am not him. I mean, I am part him, but not all. I'm like a hybrid of a demon and your dead friend. Unfortunately for you, I am in charge."

"I'm not going to beg you for my life," Kris said. "If you are going to kill me, just do it."

"Oh, I am going to kill you, but not right now. See, I need you to help me turn Harry totally evil and to stop him from fighting me like he is now. I am going to show him that if you want something the best thing to do is just take it. So you, my dear, are going to give him something that his slut of a wife couldn't."

"What is that?" Kris asked.

"A baby."

"You think you are going to keep me captive for nine months? I'll kill myself before I let that happen."

"It won't take nine months," Harry said. "It'll take until the next full moon."

"I'm not willingly going to have sex with you."

"I know," Harry said. "That's the point. The little part of Harry that is still resisting this will get to watch me rape you over and over again for the next month and then when he sees the baby he will know that my way of just taking whatever I want is the best way to live."

"So," Kris said. "That's the plan, rape me for the next month and then kill me after you get your baby?"

"Yup."

"How do you know you can even get me pregnant? I mean, you weren't man enough to knock up Janet?"

"The problem was with her, not me."

"You wish."

"No point arguing this," Harry said. "Let's get started, get on your back."

"I'm not going to let you just rape me," Kris said. "If you are going to do this, you are going to be in for a fight. You are going to have to rape a corpse."

"Don't be ridiculous," Harry said, as he opened the cage door. "I can easily overpower you."

"One day, I'll make you pay for this," Kris said. Harry threw her to the ground and began his assault. "I will kill you for this."

"Sure you will."

11

After three and a half weeks of being raped over and over again, all Kris wanted to do was die. There was no way that she was going to recover from this. She was simply waiting for the chance to be left alone long enough to figure out how to do it. It seemed that the day had finally come. Harry had just informed Kris that he was going on.

"Where you going? Let me guess, you are planning a baby shower for me and you want to invite my friends."

"Don't be silly, cops don't have any friends, now do they? But, you might be happy to know that you are in fact pregnant."

"I know, I can feel it."

"I want you to know that I will take care of the baby when you are dead and gone. It's going to be so cool to have a baby forever."

"What do you mean by that?"

"Let me explain," Harry said. "The baby will be born a mortal being on the full moon, but on the one that follows he will turn into a werewolf. By the time he reaches three years old, he will die and then become a dead the next full moon after that."

"No..."

"Yes," Harry said. "A baby dead. They really do become vicious little critters."

"You are evil."

"I'm not as evil as you think," Harry said. "Check out the side of your right breast. I know I bit you pretty hard the other night when we made love, but I sewed you up after you passed out."

"We never made love," Kris said. She looked at the sloppy stitching job that Harry had done. "You raped me."

"Come on, Kris! You can't rape the willing, and we both know that you enjoyed every bit of it."

"Fuck you."

"Kris, I don't want to fight with you. I have to go out."

"Good, go."

"By the by," Harry said. "I know that you are planning on killing yourself, but that will never happen. I will not allow it. I am going to handcuff you to the cage so that you can't climb up it and try to break your neck. That is your plan, isn't it?"

"Fuck you."

"Now, Kris, you have got to think of the baby, you are being selfish."

Kris never answered him. He let himself into her cage and roughly put her on her back. He handcuffed her to the bars, so that she would not be able to stand up. He also decided to rape her one last time, telling her that she had a nice body, for a nerdy chick.

"I'll escape when you leave and you'll never find me, or the baby," Kris said.

"No you won't," Harry said. "I should tell you, we are on a private island in the middle of Lake Rousseau. I have one snowmobile and I am taking it. So, you think you can walk across a frozen lake for miles, go ahead."

"I will."

"You won't get out of here," Harry said. "And you know it."

"I'll set off the alarm, I'm sure there is one and the cops will come."

"Yeah," Harry said. "And if they do come, I'll kill them all. You want to watch some of your friends die, Kris?"

"Fuck you."

"Yeah, that's what I thought. So, please stop with all the empty threats before you offend me."

"I wouldn't want to offend my rapist."

"No, you wouldn't."

"Before you leave, can I ask you one question?"

"Sure." Harry said, "What is it?"

"Why did you, or why did Harry, lie to me about his wife Janet? He said that he turned into a werewolf and killed her, but she is still alive."

"I know," Harry said. "I know that it was Janet that sent you over to the graveyard to kill the werewolf."

"So, why lie?"

"That's personal."

"Fuck that! You raped me and knocked me up, the least you can do is answer my fucking question!"

"Why didn't you ask her?"

"I did."

"Well, I guess she didn't feel close enough to you to answer. I'll give you a little piece of the puzzle. Harry and Janet were having troubles. He wasn't out on a romantic date with her, he was following her to see if she was cheating on him. She wasn't."

"How did she survive when he turned into a werewolf? Did he know he was going to turn, I think he said that was the first time he turned?"

"Sorry, kid. That's all I am going to tell you for now." Harry said, "Gotta go."

"Fuck you," Kris said, one last time.

Kris wondered if Harry could read her mind. She had just come up with the idea of breaking her neck by climbing up to the top of the cage and jumping down head first when he had mentioned it. She wasn't even sure if the eight foot fall would have killed her or not, but she knew she had to do something. She could not let this baby be born. Another dead was not what Muskoka needed. She had to kill this creature that was growing in her belly.

"Somebody help me!" Kris screamed. She knew it was pointless, but she had to try something. "Please help me!"

Little did Kris know, somebody was trying to help her. Harry had made it to the town of Rousseau and was sitting in a restaurant, making small talk with a blonde waitress, when his phone beeped, indicating that there was a text message waiting for him. It was from Janet.

Let her go.

Who?

Kris

No. Fuck off, bitch.

Harry, please.

Harry never bothered to answer the last text. He shut off his phone. He had made his choice. He was going to take the blonde waitress back to the island cottage and put her in the other cage. And when the full moon happened in a few days, he would lock himself in the cage with her and let the werewolf tear her to shreds before feeding on her.

It was just after dark when Harry returned with the blonde waitress. He threw her into the other cage without saying a word to Kris. He went into her cage and took off her handcuffs. He told her that she could go upstairs and get something to eat and use the bathroom, which he allowed her to do twice a day. He reminded her not to try to leave, or there would be very serious consequences.

"Who is she?" Kris asked. "Are you going to have a baby with her too?"

"No," Harry said. "She's just food for the werewolf. I don't want you to worry about her, she won't bother us. Actually, she won't make a peep. I ripped out her voice box on the way here because she wouldn't stop with the screaming."

"Inconsiderate bitch," Kris said, with a combination of sarcasm and hatred in her voice.

"Yup." Harry said, "Before you go upstairs, I should tell you that I got a message from your buddy, Janet."

"Yeah?"

"She wants me to let you go."

"Let me guess," Kris said. "You told her no."

"I told her to fuck off."

"I thought you loved her, or at least a part of you did."

"Harry is slowly coming over to my side, Kris. He doesn't care if I kill her, or you."

Kris said nothing, she went upstairs and made herself a sandwich. She went into the bathroom and showered before eating. Usually, Harry only gave her an hour, so she knew that she had to do as much as she could as quickly as possible. She sat at the kitchen table and ate. She looked outside at the snow covered hemlock trees. If they were really on an island she couldn't tell. There was too many trees blocking the view of the water and surrounding landscape.

Kris buried her hands in her face and closed her eyes. She needed to figure out how to get away from the dead, or how to kill herself. All the knives in the kitchen were plastic and there was no poison to be found anywhere. This dead was on top of things.

"God help me," Kris said.

She thought it was weird that she was asking for help from a God that she didn't believe in. She also thought it was weird when she had a quick vision of Harry talking to her back in her house before she shot him.

"If you need help you can ask God and he always helps if you are a good person."

"Okay, Harry." Kris said, "I'll do it your way until the next full moon. I'm asking God for help and I will pray to him until the next full moon."

Kris opened her eyes to see that Harry the dead was standing at the other end of the table looking down at her. He smiled at her and told her to get back in her cage.

"And just so you know, your God won't help you and he can't stop me."

Harry escorted Kris back into her cage again, but he forgot to handcuff her to the bars.

The Muskoka Monster by Patrick James

12

It came to Kris the morning before the full moon. She knew how to either escape, or make Harry kill her. She just had to time it right. The date was April the 6th and she had been held captive for almost a full month. Tonight, she either escaped, died or she gave birth to a future monster.

It was almost noon when Harry came into the basement. He looked into the other cage at the blonde waitress before turning his attention to Kris. He seemed very excited and happy about what was going to happen later in the evening. He asked Kris if there was anything that he could get her, on this her last full day of life. She told him to go fuck himself again.

"I want you to know that I have enjoyed the love making the last month," Harry said. "And I appreciate you giving your life for our baby."

"And I'd appreciate it if you'd go fuck yourself," Kris said.

"Come on, Kris! Just give in and admit that you have been defeated. All this swearing and name calling isn't going to change the fact that I beat you."

"Maybe you did and maybe you didn't."

"What does that mean?"

"You may kill me tomorrow, but according to Harry I am going to Heaven when I die because I am a good person. You will one day find yourself back in Hell again. What's it like there?"

"Maybe you'll find out tomorrow."

"Maybe, but I don't think so."

"I guess we'll just have to wait and see," Harry said. "So, is there anything that I can get you on your last day?"

"Let the girl go," Kris said. She look over at the motionless girl in the other cage.

The Muskoka Monster by Patrick James

"Oh, Kris," Harry said. "Trying to be the hero until the end."

"You asked me if I wanted you to do anything for me," Kris said. "That's what I want."

"I wish I could do that," Harry said. "But I can't. See, I need to eat tonight and it might as well be her since she is dead already."

"She's dead?" Kris asked.

"Died last night, of fright I guess. She's not the tough little bitch that you are."

"My God," Kris said.

"Again with the God stuff, Kris? Really!"

"You came from Hell and yet you don't believe in God?"

"I believe in God," Harry said. "I just don't believe he will help you. Why would he, you never gave a damn about him when things were going your way, now did you?"

"Not true," Kris said. "I never knew if he existed. All the people that told me to have faith in Him were really telling me to faith in their version of Him. I hope he understands why I didn't."

"Nah," Harry said. "I don't think he will help you. You are a nobody and you will die in the morning. Hey, do you want to know what I am going to name the baby?"

"No."

"I'm going to name him after me."

"I don't know," Kris said. "Rapist asshole is not the best name for a kid."

"No, Harry Junior, silly."

"Terrible name."

"Okay, you know what," Harry said. "I was trying to be nice to you, but if this is your attitude then I think we shouldn't talk anymore."

He turned away from Kris and left the basement. There was nothing left for her to do but wait until the full moon.

Harry returned 15 minutes before the full moon. He told Kris that she was a very lucky person because she was going to see him turn into a werewolf for a second time and not die. Most people that saw it one time never lived long enough to tell another person about it. Kris told him she was really looking forward to it.

"Really?" Harry said, "That surprises me."

"Why?"

"You want to see me tear this girl to pieces and eat her flesh?"

"No not really," Kris said. "But she is dead already, so it doesn't make that much difference, now does it?"

"It's going to be pretty graphic," Harry said. He locked himself in the other cage with the girl, using a padlock on a chain, just like the one he had on the cage that held Kris. "Really graphic."

"Yes," Kris said. "It is."

"And that doesn't bother you?"

"No because I will get my revenge in the morning."

"How so?" Harry asked.

"You'll see."

"Tell me!" Harry snapped. He was starting to change. His yellow eyes and fangs were now showing.

"Not just yet," Kris said. "Things are going to happen on my time now."

"Bitch, do not mess with me!"

"Or what, you'll kill me?" Kris said, "You're going to do that first thing tomorrow morning anyway, so there is no point threatening me."

The Muskoka Monster by Patrick James

"Tell me!" Harry screamed. The transformation into werewolf appeared to be very painful. "Tell me now!"

"Fine," Kris said. "In the morning when you return to your normal dead state, you will look over here and see me and your newly born baby."

"Damn right."

"See, but the thing is, the baby is going to be dead."

"What?" Harry asked. He had a puzzled look on his face. "What did you say?"

"After I give birth to this monster tonight," Kris rubbed her baby bump. "And you are in your helpless werewolf state, I am going to snap the baby's neck and kill it."

"Do not touch that baby!"

"It's a baby monster," Kris said. "And I am going to kill it. Hey, maybe you can eat on the next full moon."

"I will kill you!"

"Maybe, but not before I have killed the baby first," Kris said. "And there is not a damn thing you can do about it. I'm in control now, you little bitch!"

"I'll kill you!"

"Come and kill me, you douche! You kill me, you kill your baby."

Harry screamed in pain and he reached out of the cage to the spot on the floor he had left the key. He picked it up on the first try, but dropped it almost immediately. He was slowly starting to change into a werewolf and he was losing some of his ability to function.

"Problems, Harry?"

"I'll handcuff you, so that you can't kill the baby."

"Well, you had better hurry up," Kris said. "Because if you wolf out you'll just end up killing me and this little bastard I am carrying."

The Muskoka Monster by Patrick James

"You don't talk about my baby like that!"

"Oh yeah," Kris said. "What the hell are you going to do about it?"

Harry had a hard time getting himself out of the cage, but he did manage to get the chain lock off and push the door open from the inside. He ran to the cage Kris was in and shook the door. Kris called him a dumbass and told him he forgot the key. Harry spit at her and ran back to where he had left the key. Running back to the cage, he tripped and fell. Kris laughed at him. She didn't bother to tell him that he had forgotten the handcuffs.

Kris made her way to the back of the cage and watched as Harry fumbled, trying to get the lock off. When she saw the chain hit the floor, she raced at the cage door as he was opening it and rammed her shoulder into it. It hurt her shoulder, but the force was enough to knock Harry off his feet. She ran for the stairs, completely aware that she was still naked and that it was cold outside, but she had to get out of the house before he regained his senses and came after her. Unfortunately for Kris, it didn't take long for Harry to get up and come after her. She was only on the fourth stair when he grabbed her by the ankle.

"Where you going, woman?" Harry asked.

"Let go of me," Kris said. She grabbed the railing and kicked him in the face with her free foot. "I said, let go!"

"Make me, " Harry said. He threw Kris back down the stair.

"I'll make you," said a voice from behind Kris.

Harry looked up to see Janet Wilder standing on the stairs. She had an axe in her head and she used it to cut Harry's head off before he could react. She watched as Harry's head

The Muskoka Monster by Patrick James

rolled down the stairs and across the basement floor. She dropped the axe and ran to Kris.

"Are you okay, Kris?"

"I think so."

"You've got to get out of here," Janet said. "The axe is only going to delay him, he is still turning into a werewolf in a few minutes."

"Okay," Kris said. She got to her feet. "Let's go!"

"You have to go without me," Janet said. "I have to stay here."

"I'm not leaving you here with him," Kris said.

"You have to."

"Why?"

"Because I am about to turn too," Janet said. Suddenly her eyes turned yellow and fangs appeared. "You've got to go!"

The Muskoka Monster by Patrick James

"Oh no!" Kris said. She fell back on the stair. "Please, no!"

"Kris, listen to me," Janet said. "I am not going to hurt you. Not all deads stay evil, I am your friend I came to save you."

"But I thought he didn't turn you," Kris said.

"He didn't, I turned him."

"What?"

"We don't have time for this right now." Janet took off her winter coat and boots. "Put these on and go outside. You'll find my car. The lake is still frozen. Drive to my house and I'll meet you in the morning. My ownership is in the glove box, get my address from it. You believe I am your friend, don't you?"

"Yes."

"Good," Janet said. "Now get out of here! I can control the dead, but I can't control the werewolf."

The Muskoka Monster by Patrick James

"Okay," Kris said. She put the jacket and boots on. "I have to tell you, I'm pregnant."

"I know," Janet said. "We'll deal with it tomorrow, now move your ass!"

The Muskoka Monster by Patrick James

13

Kris ran to the car and hopped inside. It was already running and she didn't waste any time putting it into gear in hopes of getting as far away from the island cottage as possible. The fresh air smelled so good when she ran out the front door of the house. She wanted to enjoy it for a moment, but she knew there was no time, so she got away from there as quickly as possible.

Kris looked down at the car's speedometer. She was doing over 60 kilometers and hour, maybe too fast for the frozen lake, but she didn't know if one of the two werewolves would come after her. She cranked the car's heater and did her best to ignore the growing pain in her belly.

"Just breath, Kris," she said to herself. She looked in the glove box and found the ownership to the car. She looked at the address, a street in the area of Acton Island. She knew exactly where the place was. "Finally, a break. Of course, it would help if I knew what direction I was traveling in."

After a minute or so of driving, Kris could see the shoreline in sight. She was still about two kilometers out. She thought about how far out in the lake the island really was and how she was alone with this creature known as a dead for a month. She looked in the rear view mirror to see if a werewolf was following her. She saw nothing.

"Keep going," Kris said to herself as she listened to the sound of the ice cracking underneath the weight of the car. "Almost there, keep going."

The stomach pains were getting really severe and Kris didn't know how much more she could take. It was still really tough for her to believe that in the course of the last month, she went from not pregnant to about to spit out a monster baby. It was a nightmare that didn't seem real.

The Muskoka Monster by Patrick James

"Oh God," Kris said, as the pain of the contractions became unbearable. "I don't think I'll be able to make it any farther."

Kris had to stop on the ice and put the car into park. She unzipped the winter jacket that she got from Janet and reclined the driver's side seat. The pain was intense and she screamed in agony as she felt the baby coming. The baby she never wanted. She cried out for help, knowing that it would not be coming. She held on to the handle on the car door and pushed.

"I just want this thing out of me!" Kris cried.

The pain was so intense that she blacked out. She wasn't sure how long she was out for, but when she woke up the baby was on the floor. It was a boy. She looked for something to cut the umbilical cord with. She found a Swiss army knife in the arm rest of the car. Before she could cut the cord, she heard a huge crash on top of the car. It was one of the werewolves.

The Muskoka Monster by Patrick James

"Great," Kris said. She looked down at the baby. "Looks like one of them caught up to us."

Kris thought about it and decided that the werewolf on the roof was a blessing in disguise. If she opened the door it would get in and kill her and the baby. She would no longer have to live with the horrible memories of being kidnapped, confined and raped against her will. And the werewolf would kill the baby before it could become a dead. It seemed like a win win situation.

She reached for the door handle to open it. There was blood everywhere. Nothing compared to the amount of blood there would be when the werewolf got inside the car. She pulled back on the door release, but it didn't open. The door must have been locked. Before she could get it unlocked, Kris passed out again. When she woke up, the sun had risen and the werewolf was gone. The baby was on the passenger seat

The Muskoka Monster by Patrick James

beside her. Kris had no memory of putting him on the seat.

"Damn," Kris said. "This sucks."

She looked at the baby. It had dark hair and brown eyes and looked older than just a few hours. Must be the dead, or werewolf in it, Kris though. Kris picked it up, just to get a closer look. He tried to bite her in a very aggressive manner. She put him back down on the seat and started the car. Not sure what to do, she headed to the address on Janet's vehicle ownership.

She drove to the house, thinking about how she never saw the werewolf that had jumped on the roof of the car. She wondered if it was actually ever there, or if it was just wishful thinking on her part. It occurred to her that it might have been Janet and if it was and she had opened the door, Janet would have had to live with the memory of ripping Kris to shreds for the rest of her life. Kris realized that this wasn't fair, but at the time she was just so distraught that she would have done anything to end it all.

The house was on a nice piece of property, set back from the road. It was a big place, right on water, with a bunkie, or boat house, at the back. Kris drove up the gravel driveway, glancing sideways at the baby every now and again. She took the baby and made her way to the front door. She was relieved that the door key was on the key ring and that the baby didn't try to bite her.

Inside the house, Kris found a bedroom and put the baby on a bed. She figured that Janet wouldn't mind if she borrowed some clothes, so she helped herself and took a shower. Now, there was nothing left to do but wait for Janet to show up and tell her how to get out of this mess. What Kris didn't know was that Janet wouldn't show up until the next day.

Kris made her way back into the bedroom. She wondered if she should

The Muskoka Monster by Patrick James

feed the baby something. No, she didn't want it to live, but until she worked up the courage to kill it, she didn't want to be cruel. But then again, she wasn't going to be stupid either. The way the baby tried to bite her earlier guaranteed that she was not going to let it breastfeed from her.

She went into the kitchen and tried to call Janet's cell from the home's land line. She got no answer and with every single time she got voicemail her stress level rose higher. Was Janet dead? Did Harry kill her?

The truth was Janet was fine. She had already made her way off the island. She wanted to go see Kris, but she had something else to do first. Something was bothering her and she had to go investigate. Janet had figured that there was only one person that could have stolen Harry's body before it was buried and she wanted to go confront him. She met him in a very isolated area.

In actual fact, it wasn't a person that she was going to confront, it was a dead. The only other dead living in the Muskoka area. Janet hadn't seen him in person in years, but he did come to her in dreams on occasion, just like he did with Harry.

"Did you steal Harry's body from the funeral home?" Janet asked.

"Yes."

"May I ask why?"

"I don't know why," the dead answered. "It was just an impulse I acted on."

"Come on," Janet said. "There's more to it than that."

"You really want to know?"

"I do."

"Fine. I wanted to see if Harry would be more grateful for the gift of being a dead then you were. You always treated it like it was a bad thing, I wanted to see if he would."

"But you didn't create him," Janet said. "You created me and I created him."

"That has nothing to do with it, Janet. You've had a century and a half of living as a dead, shouldn't Harry get his chance too?"

"No."

"Why not? He's no threat to you."

"He's a threat to human beings."

"That's their problem, isn't it? Why would you try to protect them from one of your own? You know what humans would want to do to you if they knew what you were."

"He raped the girl."

"No, he mated with her."

"Against her will."

The Muskoka Monster by Patrick James

"She's a lesser species, what she wants doesn't matter."

"You were a human once."

"Twenty-five hundred years ago, but I have evolved since then."

"Well," Janet said. "I should be going. This argument isn't going to get us anywhere."

"Before you run off, I need to tell you a couple things that I might know that you don't."

"Okay."

"First thing is, Harry called me this morning and I told him about your house on Acton Island. And I told him that Kris is there with the baby."

"Why would you do that?"

"Second thing is, I need to slow you down for a day or two, so that he can make his way to her."

The ancient dead produced a gun and emptied into Janet's head and chest. She would need a full twenty-four hours to recover from her wounds.

The Muskoka Monster by Patrick James

14

Kris gave in and fed the baby some oatmeal she found in the kitchen. It made the baby look at her with some affection, which was weird for her. She knew what it was going to become and she knew that she couldn't allow that to happen, but then there was the other side of it, the fact that this baby had no say in what it was going to become. It wasn't fair.

It was chilly inside the house, so Kris went into the living room and fired up the wood burning fireplace. She held the baby in her arms, as she looked at the flames. It would be so easy just to throw the baby in the flames and end it all. Physically easy, not emotionally easy. Either way, she couldn't do it.

"Maybe Janet can do it when she gets here," Kris said to herself. She took the baby to the bedroom and put it back on the bed. "What the hell am I saying! I can't let her do that.

Like it, or not I am not just going to allow my baby to be murdered."

"I'm glad to hear that." Kris turned around to see Harry Wilder standing in the doorway of the bedroom. He smiled at her. "I knew you'd come around."

"How did you find me?"

"Mental connection with the baby, Harry lied. "I have to give it to you, Kris. You are a fighter."

"Can you do me a favour," Kris said. "On the sofa there is a teddy bear. Can you get it for me?"

"Sure," Harry said. He tried hard to hide his surprise at how civil Kris was being with him. He walked into the living room and found the stuffed toy. He picked it up and took it into the bedroom and handed it to Kris. "Here you go."

"Thanks," Kris said.

"So, your original plan was to ask Janet to kill the baby."

"Yeah, I figured she owed me. She asked me to go to your grave and kill you, or at least you in werewolf form. I agreed to do it because she was too close to you."

"So, you feel close to the baby."

"I didn't want to," Kris admitted. "And I still haven't forgiven you for raping me, but yes I feel close to him."

"That's too bad," a voice coming from behind Kris and Harry said. It was Janet. "Because it has to die."

"Bitch," Harry said. "I will end you."

"Kind of hard to do, tough guy."

"Janet, where have you been?" Kris asked.

"It doesn't matter, I'm here now."

The Muskoka Monster by Patrick James

"I know where you were," Harry said.

"Good for you," Janet replied. "Hand me the baby, Kris. It is going in the fire."

"No," Kris said. "I can't.

"The baby is coming with me, right now," Harry said. He picked the baby up. "Kris, don't try to stop me. I promise you I will raise the baby and I will not let any harm come to him."

"Harm is coming right now," Janet said. She stepped forward.

"No," Kris said. She jumped in front of Harry and the baby. "Don't!"

"Kris, that baby is dangerous, it's going to turn into a werewolf and then a dead. Is that what you want?"

"I know it isn't ideal, but it is still my baby and I don't want to kill it."

"You don't have to," Janet said. "I'll do it."

"No," Kris said. "I mean, I don't want it to die."

"But it's going to turn evil."

"There are lots of human babies that will be evil when they grow up and we don't kill them."

"That's a bullshit justification and you know it," Janet said. "We can't tell what human babies are going to be evil, but in the case of this baby, we know one hundred percent that it will be."

"Ladies," Harry said. "I don't know how this will factor into the decision here, but there is something you should both know."

"Yeah, what's that?" Janet asked.

"I came here to kill Kris," Harry said. "But I have had a change of heart. Seeing how she doesn't want our baby to die, I am willing to leave her alone and never harm her as long as she stays away and doesn't come after me, or the kid."

"You won't kill her because I'll stop you," Janet said.

"If we fight right now," Harry said. "You might stop me, and then again you might not. But can you say for sure that you will always be there to stop me? If you let me walk out of here, I'll leave you and her alone."

"I wish I could do that," Janet said. "But I can't."

"Janet, please!" Kris sounded very emotional. "Last night you told me that you were my friend and I didn't have to be afraid of you."

"You don't."

"You also said that you would never hurt me."

"Yeah," Janet said. "What's your point?"

"If you kill my son, that hurts me."

"She's got you there," Harry said.

The Muskoka Monster by Patrick James

"You shut up!" Janet said, "Kris, are you sure this is what you want?"

"Yes."

"Fine," Janet sighed. "Against my better judgement, I will let Harry walk out of here."

"Promise me that you will never go after him, or the baby," Kris said.

"Kris...."

"Promise me!" Kris yelled.

"Fine," Janet answered. "I promise, I will never go after Harry, or your baby. Happy?"

"I don't know about her," Harry said. "But I am delighted."

"Step aside, please Janet," Kris said. "Let them leave."

Janet moved out of the doorway and left enough room for Harry to exit. Harry took a step towards the door when Kris called him back. She handed him the teddy bear, with tears rolling down her face, and told Harry it was the kid's favourite toy. Harry took it without saying anything to Kris. As he got close to Janet, he told her that he had to "borrow" her car because it was too cold for the baby to be outside.

Kris and Janet watched Harry walk out the front door with the baby in his arms. There didn't seem to be anything to say. Kris locked herself in a bedroom for a few hours, before coming out to talk to Janet.

"Harry thought I was cheating," Janet said. "Because I would always take off once a month and he wouldn't see me for a day, or two."

"I know," Kris said. "He told me he followed you."

"Yeah," Janet said. "I have a couple different hiding places that I go to when I wolf out."

"You know what's weird," Kris said. "You two don't seem like you like each other much now, but when he was in my police car he talked with so much love about you."

"That's what happens when you turn into a dead," Janet said. "The bad feelings take over. He's mad at me for not telling him my dirty secret, that I am an almost two hundred year old werewolf slash dead, I'm mad at him for not trusting me and following me. I mean, he should have known that I would never cheat and he should have just left me alone. Let me have my me time."

"I guess everybody has secrets," Kris said. "But yours was a big one."

"Yeah," Janet said. "You know, I wish Harry could get more control over that dead that is walking around in his body. If he could only see the fact that I protected him from not only the werewolf, but the dead, he would know how much I truly loved him. Most deads see human beings as meals, or a means to reproduce, not as equals."

"This dead versus you thing confuses me," Kris said. "Like right now, what are you? Are you Janet, or are you the dead?"

"I'm Janet, of course. I control the dead, but I have to live with it because if it dies, so do I."

"Does it still talk to you, like the dead that talked to Harry?"

"Oh yeah," Janet laughed. "And mine hates me.

"How did you do it?" Kris asked. "How did you get control of it?"

"Before I was turned," Janet said. "I was a very religious person. Of course, back in the 1800's, most of us were."

"It's so cool to be talking to somebody that was alive in the old days."

"It's unnatural though," Janet said. "I was turned into a dead when I was thirty-two years old. I was born in 1830, I shouldn't be here in the 2010's. Most people born up here in the 1830's never even got to see 1900."

"Oh, I see where this is going," Kris said. "This is about me killing you on the next full moon when you turn into a werewolf."

"No," Janet said. "I won't ask you to do that. You have already been through enough, however if you wanted to do me that favour I would be grateful."

"Thank God."

"Which brings me back to the original point of this conversation," Janet said. "How I got the dead under control. One morning, after a full moon, I was covered in the blood of my latest victim and making my way home, when I came across my old church. The building was in ruins, the town I am from no longer exists, there are a few buildings left, but most of them have been knocked down, when the province ran Highway 11 through there. Anyway, I went into my old church and sat there."

"How long had it been since you had been there?"

"This was 1970," Janet said. "So, over a hundred years."

"Wow," Kris said.

"It was the strangest thing in my life," Janet said. "Even weirder than being turned into a werewolf. I sat there and I thought about all the family and friends that I use to talk with after Sunday service and how they were all dead and gone. Hopefully, most of them are in Heaven now. And then I did something I had not done since I had been turned into a dead."

"What?" Kris asked.

"I cried. Didn't even know that it was possible for my kind. I actually felt sadness and guilt, things deads don't feel. So, I took that moment to drop to my knees and beg God to free me from this thing. When I left, I was able to actually touch a Bible again and I began reading it again. I pray every night."

"That's great," Kris said. "But go back to when you were in the church. When you asked God for help, did he answer you?"

"Yes," Janet said. "He told me that he would send somebody to help me."

"You actually heard him say the words, I will send somebody to help you?"

"No," Janet said. "It was more of a vision."

"What kind of vision?"

"He showed me the person that was going to help me," Janet said. "A person I had never met."

"Really."

"Yes, Kris. He showed me you."

"Me?"

"Yes."

"Holy frigging shit," Kris said. "That is so trippy."

"You really do have a way with words," Janet said, with a smile. "You should write a book or something."

15

Harry had spent his first month as a parent and he was loving it. It was May now and soon, the city idiots from Toronto and the suburbs would start coming up to Muskoka to their summer homes. He would have many potential new victims and many new potential meals at his disposal. All, he had to do was get through this next full moon.

He put the baby, Harry Jr., in his own separate cage. He didn't like it, but he knew that his werewolf would attack and kill the baby werewolf. It was only for one night. Harry locked himself in his own cage and eyed his meal, a young woman that he had met and kidnapped from an isolated cottage. She was perfect because she had an infant child that was just the perfect size for Junior to feast on during his first werewolf turning. Both mother and baby had already been killed by Harry. He did enjoy killing and eating his victims fresh, when he wolfed out, but this was a private moment between father and son. He didn't want anybody else to witness it, even if they would die soon after.

It didn't take Harry long to figure out he could use the fact that women can't resist babies to his advantage. He had noticed the young woman one day when he was out looking for his werewolf's next meal. She was driving a little compact car and with his dead eyes he could see that she had a baby in the car with her. Two for one shopping.

He followed her completely and totally unnoticed to her tiny, remote cottage. He didn't do anything that day. He spent the next week watching her. She seemed to be alone. Not that it mattered, he could kill anybody he wanted to.

On the day he decided to move in on her, he decided to be a bit more creative than usual. Before Harry Jr. was in his life, he would have kicked in the door, slapped the bitch around,

The Muskoka Monster by Patrick James

killed the baby to show her he wasn't messing around and then he would drag her ass out of the cottage and back to the cage of his choosing.

He knew her schedule, and he knew that she came home around four every afternoon. A single mother with no education, working at a greasy spoon to raise a bastard child. Life must suck for her, Harry thought. He would be doing her a favour if he ended her miserable existence.

"People like her mean nothing to this world, Junior. They are useless. Let's give her a purpose and her baby too. They can be our next meal."

Harry parked the car that he stole from Janet on the road in front of the young woman's house. He shut it off and then lifted the hood like it had broken down. As she was pulling up to her house, she saw Harry pacing in front of the car while holding the baby in a blanket. Immediately, she offered to help and told him that he could borrow her phone to call for help. Once inside her house, Harry attacked immediately. She never stood a chance.

Now, the woman was dead inside a cage with Harry and her baby was dead inside a cage with Harry Jr. Harry sat in the cage, waiting to wolf out. He had a camera set up, so that he could watch his son turning for the first time over and over again.

The cottage was a new one, just outside of Huntsville on Fairy Lake. Harry felt pretty secure in it, as nobody knew that he was there. At least that is what he thought. What he didn't know was that trouble had just arrived outside the cottage in the form of Janet Wilder and Kris Speers.

"We've got to hurry," Janet said to Kris, as she put the car in park. "I'm about to turn soon."

"Don't badger me," Kris said. "I know."

The Muskoka Monster by Patrick James

"Let's do this," Janet said. She ran at the front door and hit it with her shoulder. The door flew open to reveal Harry sitting in his cage. He looked startled when he saw Janet standing there. "Hello, Harry."

Janet ran to the cage that Harry Jr. was locked in and picked up the key for the lock off the floor. Harry screamed at her to get away from the baby and ran to the door of the cage holding him. Before he could get to the key, Kris Speers came running into the cottage with a gun in her hand. She shot Harry in the chest. He wasn't killed, of course, as he was still a dead for another few minutes, but it did slow him down. He was on his back cursing the pair of them, when Janet got the lock open and got into the cage with the baby.

"Lock it up," Janet yelled to Kris. She locked Janet in with the baby. "You ready?"

"As I will ever be," Kris said.

"Remember," Janet said. "There is one other dead in Muskoka and he will not be happy with you. Once you have killed all three of us, I want you to get the hell out of here and never come back ever. If you do, he will kill you."

"Got it."

"Go to Halifax," Janet said. "I have a friend there, I left her contact info on your phone. She'll help you get a new identity and she'll set you up with enough money that you'll never have to worry again."

"Okay," Kris said. "I got it. I'm still not happy about any of this."

"Hey, I'll see you again," Janet said. "In Heaven."

"That's funny!" Harry had managed to sit up, although he was covered in blood. "You're a demon, you are evil, you aren't going to Heaven."

The Muskoka Monster by Patrick James

"Yes, I am Harry. I made things right with God. You can too, it's never too late."

"We had a deal, Kris." Harry said, "I thought you had honour."

"I do," Kris said. "But I also have a sense of right and wrong and I was never going to let you live."

"Or your baby?"

"Don't you get it?" Kris asked. "Janet and I set you up. She called me the morning after your last change. It was all a plan. I never loved that baby, it's evil and I want it dead. I would never stand by and let innocent people die because of my child."

"You bitch..."

"I'm a smart bitch, though." Kris said, "Actually, we're both smart bitches. We knew that you would steal Janet's car because you are such a douche, so when you were in the house talking to me, she planted a tracking system. I also put one in the teddy bear. It was so easy. All we had to do was wait for the next full moon."

"I'll kill you!"

"You don't get it, you have lost!"

"You'll lose," Harry snapped. "You can't kill me, you can only send me back to Hell. But, I will get out again and when I do, I will kill you."

"Ask God for forgiveness, Harry!" Janet screamed. "Repent!"

"Go to hell, bitch!"

There was a loud scream from behind Janet. She turned to see that the baby had already turned into a mini werewolf. It jumped at her face, but she swatted it away with no effort. Kris calmly raised the gun and pointed it at the baby werewolf. With it locked in her sights, she pulled the trigger. The silver bullet hit it right between the eyes. There was a sudden burst of flame and within a few seconds the baby werewolf was reduced to ashes.

"No!!!" Harry cried, "What kind of a monster kills her own baby?"

"You're next," Kris said. She sounded like she meant business.

"Actually," Janet interrupted. "I think I am next. I feel myself changing."

"I'm going to miss you," Kris said.

"I'll miss you too, but we will meet again," Janet said. "Thanks for doing this."

"Thanks for all your help," Kris said. "I had nobody to turn to and I wouldn't have made it without you."

"Harry!" Janet said. "Please forgive me! I wasn't keeping secrets from you to harm you. I was trying to protect you. Let go of the anger."

Harry couldn't answer. He had already begun to turn. The whole transformation thing was just as frightening to Kris as it had been the first time. She looked from Janet to Harry to see which one was going to turn first. Listening to Janet scream in pain as she turned into a werewolf was very emotionally stressful for Kris. Kris watched the last few moments of Janet turning without looking at Harry. When Janet had totally changed, Kris pointed the gun at her and pulled the trigger.

"See you in Heaven," Kris said.

She watched as fire turned Janet's body into ashes. She turned to face Harry and saw that he had completely wolfed out and was ramming the cage door, in an attempt to get to her. She raised the gun and pulled the trigger.

It was over.

Kris took a minute to gather her thoughts. She knew that she had done the right thing and that the world was a better and safer place than it would have been had she not pulled the trigger three times. Still, the taking of three lives was not an easy thing.

The Muskoka Monster by Patrick James

"Guess I'm not just a traffic cop anymore," Kris said. She left the cottage and made her way to the car. "God, give me the strength to get on with my life after this."

She started up the car and waited for it to warm up. At least that is what she told herself. It was early in the month of May and the weather was warm now. Her hands were still shaking as she put the car in gear and drove away from the cottage. She was headed for the police station to hand in her weapon and badge. She knew that her father would understand, so she wasn't going to leave him the usual letter of resignation. She hoped he wasn't at the station when she showed up. They had never really been that close, but she didn't want to look at him again, knowing that it would be the last time she would ever see him in her life. He was still her father and the only family she had. No, it would be better if she could just drop off her stuff in his office and leave.

The Muskoka Monster by Patrick James

"I killed the only friends I had," Kris said to herself. She had really liked Harry before he wolfed out and came back as a dead. The real Harry was a good guy. And Janet was just a cool chick. "Not looking forward to spending the rest of my life alone in some strange city."

Kris was relieved to see that her dad wasn't in his office. She was in and out of the office, with nobody but the dispatcher even noticing her. The dispatcher was an angry woman and never spoke to anybody unless she had to. Generally, Kris didn't care for her, but was very happy that she was on duty this night.

"See you, Muskoka," Kris said as she started the car and headed over to Highway 11. "I never wanted to leave here."

16

Chief Speers would not get his daughter's badge and weapon until the next morning. He woke up on the floor of a prison cell, naked and covered in blood. He had been greedy and feed on two people this full moon. A couple of homeless meth heads he had arrested for breaking into an empty cottage. They had no identification on them and there likely wasn't anybody looking for them, so he took them back to the station and put them in his private cell in the basement. It was the perfect place to turn because the basement was only accessible from his office and nobody knew it was there.

The Chief got dressed after he used his private shower in his office. He sat at his desk and looked at his daughter's badge. He wasn't sad that she was gone, in fact he was quite relieved. It wasn't that he didn't love her, it was just tough to keep a secret like his away from a family member that he saw every single day.

The Muskoka Monster by Patrick James

And there was another secret that he was surprised that Janet had not shared with Kris. Chief Speers had told Kris that her mother had been killed by a drunk driver. It wasn't true. The truth was, her mother was just some random woman that he had kidnapped and raped until he got a baby. After the baby was born, he fed on the mother the next full moon.

"My darling daughter," Speers said. "You don't know how rare you are. The only baby I have ever heard of that was born to a dead and yet never turned into a werewolf, or a dead. It is unheard of."

The chief figured that Janet would have come completely clean with Kris, if she really wanted to clear her conscience. He really thought she was going to tell his daughter that he was the other dead living in the Muskoka area. Of course, if she had done that, Chief Speers would have been left with no choice, but to murder his very own daughter. He didn't want to do that, but Janet had given up to many secrets of the dead and the chief could not allow anybody with the knowledge of how to kill him live. It just wasn't practical. He had always been a bit afraid of Kris, even if he didn't like to admit having fear of anything.

"I always wondered if there was something supernatural involved with Kristine," Chief Speers said. He got up and walked over to the window of his office and looked out at the parking lot. He talked to himself on a regular basis. "I always wondered if God, or some angel blessed her and turned her into something special, something more than just a regular human being."

Now, she was gone and it was a relief. Still, he felt kind of sad. He was alone again, no family and no friends. He had hoped that Janet would have been more loyal to him and that they would have stayed together as friends forever. The ungrateful bitch had ruined everything.

The Muskoka Monster by Patrick James

Maybe it was time to move on. He could kill off Chief Speers and just reinvent himself as somebody else. Muskoka had been home to him for a long time, and he loved it, but there was a big world out there and maybe it was time to go see another part of it. He knew that his daughter was going to take on a new identity, so why not do the exact same thing?

"A new identity to hide from me, like I would kill her!" The Chief said, "Maybe I should kill her, she did kill three werewolves and one of them was my grandson. A grandson I never got to even meet. Sure, I love her, but she did betray me. I don't know, I'll have to think about it."

He wondered where Kris was going to move to and if he should eventually try to find her. It might make sense to keep an eye on her, he thought, and see if she goes after other werewolves in her new location. If she does, it might be smart to kill her. If she doesn't, he could just watch her for a

The Muskoka Monster by Patrick James

few months and make sure she was okay. He worried about her and wanted her to be happy, as long as she wasn't a threat to him.

"Nobody should have to go through life without a family."

Going through life without having any family with her was exactly what Kris Speers would have to do. Except that she wasn't Kris Speers anymore. Janet's friend had gotten her a new identity, as promised, and set her up with a lot of money. She even got a new job working for Canada Customs as customs officer at the port authority.

Halifax was a major port on the east coast for ships coming from all over the world and going all over the world. Cruise ships and freightliners were in and out all day and night every day of the year.

Her name was Vicki Moore now. It was January and she had been living in Halifax for around eight months. She worked the night shift five days a

The Muskoka Monster by Patrick James

week and was basically a glorified security guard now. She didn't have to work, she had millions of dollars in the bank, but she decided it was better to do something other than just sit around the house all day. She still wasn't comfortable living on the east coast and longed for her old house in Muskoka. She would go to the websites of all the Muskoka newspapers and read up on all the latest news. Three months ago, she was devastated when she had read that her father had died of an apparent heart attack.

It was tough to get over his death without any friends to help comfort her. One thing that hadn't changed since she left Ontario was that she still had trouble connecting with other people. The only person she ever talked to was her new partner on the night shift, a guy named Jason Perry.

He seemed like a nice enough guy, but he wasn't that chatty. He was older than her, maybe forty-five with ginger hair and a stocky build. He was

The Muskoka Monster by Patrick James

shorter than her too, which didn't seem to bother him, but she would have preferred a taller partner. Just once she wanted to have a male partner that she was sexually attracted to, just to see if it would go anywhere, but it wasn't going to happen this time.

Halifax got a lot of snow in the winter, maybe even more than Central Ontario. And the wind that came off the Atlantic Ocean was brutally cold.

It was January 26th, a Thursday and the second to last day of work for Vicki. After these last two shifts, she would have four much needed days off. She left for work an hour earlier because Jason had asked her to do him a favour and come out to his house in the suburbs to pick him up. He drove this old beat up truck that had been giving him some problems lately. She had tried to talk him into spending some money and leasing a newer vehicle, but he told her that he was proud to be cheap.

The Muskoka Monster by Patrick James

So, off she went to the middle of nowhere to pick up a guy she hadn't known very long, during a really cold and snowy night. Jason's house was a smaller bungalow on a large lot. It reminded her of her old house in Muskoka and it made her feel homesick for a moment. She fought of the sad feeling and went and knocked on the front door. Jason answered and invited her in.

"We should go soon," Vicki said. "The roads are pretty bad."

"We will," Jason said. "Just brewing some coffee. Want a cup to go? I've got a couple travel mugs."

"Sure," Vicki said. "It'll save us time if we don't have to stop."

"That's what I was thinking."

"Hey, did you get the new police boots delivered yet?"

"Got the boots and bullet proof vests too," Jason said. "But I haven't had time to go through them. I was

The Muskoka Monster by Patrick James

thinking maybe I'll wait until spring before I wear mine. Nothing worse than the road salts messing up a new pair of boots."

"I know," Vicki said. "But this pair that I am wearing are killing my feet."

"Can you get through another night? I mean, I haven't even opened the box yet."

"Or I could just grab them real quick," Vicki said. "While you pour our coffee."

"Sure," Jason said. We went into the kitchen cabinet and took out a steak knife. He slid it across the counter to her. "The box is in the basement. How do you take your coffee, double/double, right?"

"Yeah," Vicki said. "I'll be right back."

"Before you go I have to tell you something, Kris. I won't be at work tomorrow night, so you'll have to work solo. I have to take a personal day."

"Okay."

Vicki made her way down into the basement of the old house. It had a moldy smell and was very dark. Jason had told her that she would have to make her way to the basement in the dark, but when she got to the bottom of the stairs, she would find a light bulb with a pull string to turn it on. She had no problem getting to the bottom of the stairs in the dark, she had eyes like a bat from working so many night shifts in her life. As she reached up for the pull string, she had a cold chill run down her spine. It took a moment for it to register with her, but Jason, her new partner, had just called her Kris, not Vicki. As she turned on the light, she heard footsteps coming down the steps towards her.

"I'm sorry, Kris," Jason said. "I screwed up. I didn't want you to find out who I was so quickly."

The Muskoka Monster by Patrick James

"Who are you?" Kris said, "I know what you are, but I don't know who you are."

"It's a full moon tomorrow night," Jason said. "That's why I can't come into work. That's why I'll be locked up in that."

Jason pointed at a cage at the far end of the basement. There was a woman locked inside of it. Kris couldn't believe what was happening to her. She wasn't scared anymore, she was way beyond that now. She simply wanted answers.

"So where do I know you from?"

"You don't recognize me?"

"No, should I?"

"Look at my eyes," Jason said. "I mean really look. Study them."

"Dad?" Kris said, as she stared into the dead's eyes. "Is that you?"

"Yes," Jason said. "It is."

The Muskoka Monster by Patrick James

The Muskoka Monster by Patrick James

Author's comments

Five or six years ago, I was up in Bracebridge for a mini vacation. One night, as I looked around at the very rugged landscape and all wilderness around me, I had a thought. This would be the perfect setting for a werewolf novel. It helped that there was a full moon that night.

I struggled for a few years on how to make a werewolf novel unique and different. I mean, vampires can have their own unique personalities, but a werewolf is a werewolf and they are pretty much all the same. Eventually, I came up with the idea that the infected werewolf would remember everything that happened and be forced to watch it kill. The idea for the creature known as a dead came as I was writing.

Initially, I thought the werewolf would represent anger and rage, but it quickly became apparent to me that this werewolf was all about secrets. I've been writing for years and it still baffles me how the character take over a story and basically write the book for you. Sometimes I feel like a glorified typist.

I hope you enjoyed the book and if you are interested in future projects you can find my blog at:

http://authorpatrickjames.blogspot.ca/

The Muskoka Monster by Patrick James

Made in the USA
Middletown, DE
03 January 2020